L E G E N

O F

LADY ILENA

ALSO AVAILABLE IN DELL LAUREL-LEAF BOOKS

THE SEER AND THE SWORD, *Victoria Hanley*

LUCY THE GIANT, *Sherri L. Smith*

THE RAG AND BONE SHOP, *Robert Cormier*

WHEN ZACHARY BEAVER CAME TO TOWN, *Kimberly Willis Holt*

FREEDOM BEYOND THE SEA, *Waldtraut Lewin*

LORD OF THE DEEP, *Graham Salisbury*

LORD OF THE NUTCRACKER MEN, *Iain Lawrence*

THE GADGET, *Paul Zindel*

SHATTERED MIRROR, *Amelia Atwater-Rhodes*

SHADES OF SIMON GRAY, *Joyce McDonald*

THE LEGEND OF LADY ILENA

by

Patricia Malone

Published by
Dell Laurel-Leaf
an imprint of
Random House Children's Books
a division of Random House, Inc.
New York

Visit us on the Web! www.randomhouse.com/teens

Educators and librarians, for a variety of teaching tools, visit us at
www.randomhouse.com/teachers

ISBN: 0-440-22909-X

RL: 4.9

Reprinted by arrangement with Delacorte Press

Printed in the United States of America

July 2003

10 9 8 7 6 5 4 3

OPM

For Irene

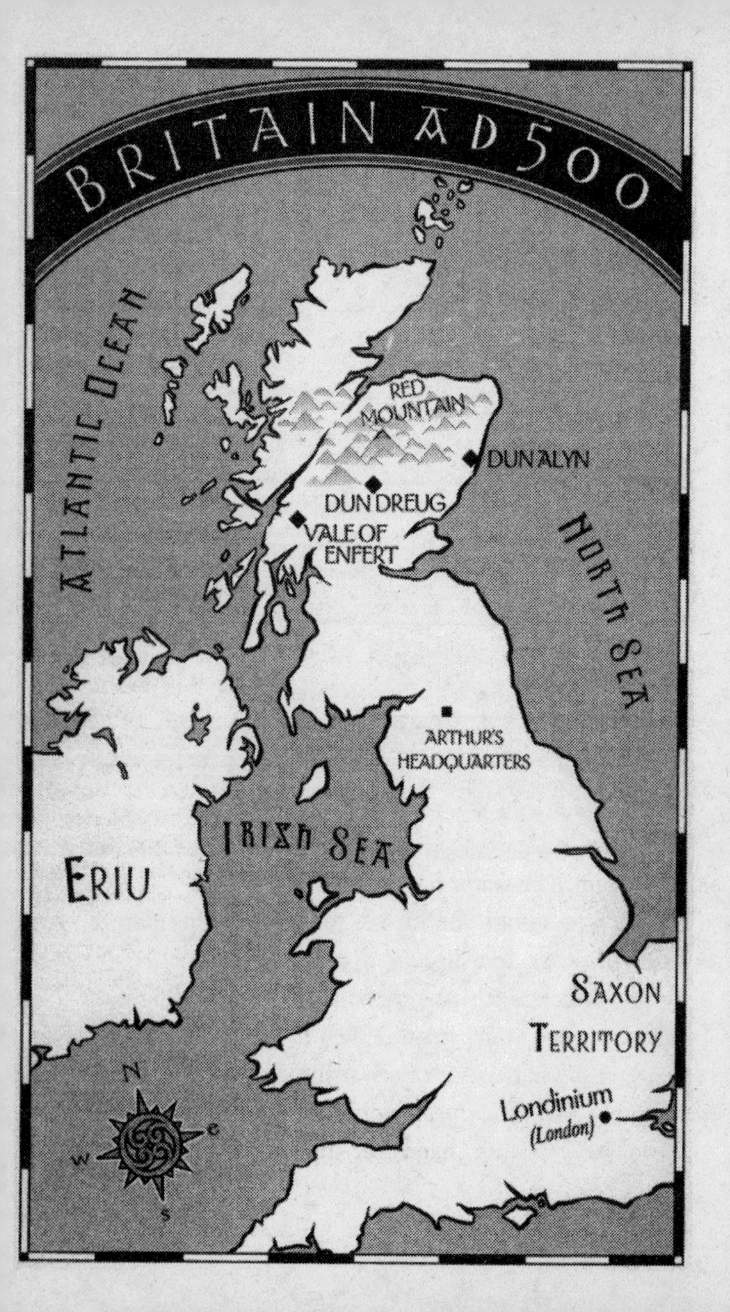

BRITAIN AD 500
ATLANTIC OCEAN
RED MOUNTAIN
DUNALYN
DUN DREUG
VALE OF ENFERT
NORTH SEA
ARTHUR'S HEADQUARTERS
IRISH SEA
ERIU
SAXON TERRITORY
Londinium
(London)
N
E
W
S

CHAPTER

1

"ILENA? ARE YOU THERE?"

The low stool he made for me when I was a child is near his bedplace. I pull it closer and sit beside him.

"I'm here, Moren. What is it?"

"My dream. I saw the hag at streamside."

I feel a chill despite the warm fall sunlight flooding through the open door. "No! Do not think of that. I've sent for Aten. She'll bring stronger herbs."

"It's too late. The old woman washed my clothes in the stream. The water ran red with my blood."

I try to sound confident. "Aten will help. Have a drink of water. Your lips are dry from fever."

My father clutches at my hand with a fumbling motion that tears at my heart. When he is well, his wrists bulge with the muscles of a warrior. He trained me day after day, year after year, until I too could swing the sword with either hand for hours. "Stamina, lass, stamina!" he would say as we practiced. "The battle goes to those who hold out until their opponents falter."

It is agony for me to watch him now that he is weak and helpless, dependent on me to hold the bowl of water, to wipe his face, and to bring the slop jar. I lift his shoulders so that he can sip, then lay him back gently and take his hand in mine.

"I saw her clearly," he says.

Sudden tears blur my vision, and I swipe at them with my free hand. When a warrior dreams of the old woman at the stream, death is near.

Cryner lets out a warning bark from his sunny spot by the front door.

"Ilena?" It's Aten's voice from the path.

I put Moren's hand down on the bedskins and hurry outside.

Aten is the village healer. She and her husband helped us when my parents rode their tired horses over the snow-laden pass into this valley fifteen years ago. I was only a few days old, wrapped tightly against my mother's chest, weak with hunger because her milk wasn't strong enough yet to sustain me. It was Aten who put me to breast at once and saved my life.

Her son, Jon, was two when we came. Her daughter, Fiona, was born a year after we arrived. They are my closest friends in the village, and I'm glad to see that Fiona is with her now.

Cryner greets them and thrusts his head against Fiona's skirt until she stoops to scratch his long hound ears. She pushes him away when he tries to lick her face, and he goes back to resume his nap.

Aten carries her small iron pot filled with medicines. She takes out a handful of plants and three cloth bundles, then hands me the empty kettle. "Get water heating, Ilena. Half-full will do. I'll put these inside where the wind won't take them, and I'll have a look at Moren." She disappears into the house.

"Is it bad?" Fiona is already stirring the outside fire into a blaze.

"I fear so," I answer. "He speaks of seeing the crone at the stream."

She shakes her head. "Not a good sign, that."

I dip water from the barrel by the door and hang the pot over the hottest part of the fire. "I'm glad you came," I say. "I heard the boys return from gathering wood and hailed them. I hoped they would get the message to you quickly."

"Aye. Nol's son ran ahead of the others to tell us, and we left at once."

Aten's face is grim when she comes out of the house. She jostles the iron kettle as if to urge it to heat faster before she turns to me. "His lungs are badly congested. When did he get home?"

"Just before sunset yesterday," I reply. "I heard him coming and ran out to meet him. He was slumped over his horse's neck and could not raise himself enough to greet me. I caught him as he slid from the saddle, and I could feel the fever.

"I got him into his bedplace and prepared a strong tea of pennyroyal and thyme. It lowered the fever, but he would not eat. He slept fitfully through the night and seemed no better this morning."

Aten jostles the pot again and watches steam begin to rise. She says, "I'll mix something stronger. It may loosen his breathing."

"The trip to the East again?" Fiona asks.

I nod. "It was difficult for him last year, and I begged him not to go this time. But he said that he was expected."

"He has aged in the two years since Grenna died," Aten says.

I look up to the hill above the house. I can see the cairn that we built on my mother's grave. I wonder how long it will be before another is raised beside it to mark my father's resting place. I blink back tears.

Aten puts her arms around me. "Do not weep, Ilena. We'll work hard to help him."

"Tell her about the dream," Fiona says.

"The death dream of a warrior," I say. "He saw the crone."

"We'll not give up yet." Aten too looks toward my mother's grave before she carries the hot water into the house.

They stay with me through the afternoon, but I shake my head when Fiona offers to spend the night. "Thank you, but I will be fine."

"Are you sure?" Aten asks.

"You have your own chores. Come in the morning when you can," I say, "and thank you."

Fiona lingers at the door when Aten leaves. "I could keep you company."

I walk out into the yard with her. "I know you plan to go to the singing," I say.

On summer evenings the other young people meet in a grove of trees near the end of the valley. I can hear the pipes and sometimes the laughter from up here on the slope. When we were small, I often joined Jon and Fiona. We would lurk about with the other children, spying on courting couples and dancing in our own little circles.

As I grew older, Jon's attentions toward me changed, and Moren found more and more reasons why I should stay at home in the evenings. When I became a woman, he forbade me to go to the singings at any time.

"Your destiny is not in this valley, lass," he said when I complained, but he would not explain what he meant.

Fiona says, "Of course I was planning to go, but I will stay here if you need me."

"I thank you for offering, but there is one who would miss you if you did not appear at the gathering."

She smiles and her cheeks flush. "Yes, he would," she says, "but we'll have many years together."

"Is it settled then?" I can't imagine choosing someone to live with forever.

She nods. "My father has agreed. We'll be married in the spring." She hesitates, then says, "Are you sure you will not consider Jon? My brother is a fine man."

"Yes, he is," I say. "And he is my friend. But I am not ready for marriage."

"But you are older than I." She shakes her head.

I was trained to be a warrior, not a wife. While Fiona danced and sang at the evening gatherings, I played at sword fighting with Moren. While she learned to weave and spin, I rode out of the valley to hunt deer and wild boar. Grenna took care that I learned about the herbs for healing, which wild plants were edible and which poisonous, and how to keep the stew pot from burning our food, but I spent little time on household tasks.

Often, as I watched Fiona stroll along the stream, picking green shoots for dinner, or walk with friends into the woods to gather nuts, I longed to lay down my heavy shield, put my sword away, and join her.

But Moren was always firm. "Our people are warriors, Ilena. Your responsibilities are far greater than those of your friends. You must be prepared."

Cryner has come to the gate with us. He nuzzles Fiona until she scratches his ears again.

"I know I'm old enough to marry," I say, "but there are places I want to see, things I must know before I settle down with a husband."

She sighs and hugs me. "Goodbye then, and may your god be with you this night."

I stand by the gate and watch while she catches up with her mother; then I turn back to the house.

The three of us made our own life here a little apart from the village, near the trail that leads over the mountain pass to the outside world. We were welcome at any fire in the settlement, but no one, least of all my parents, ever forgot that we came from someplace else and never truly belonged in the Vale of Enfert.

Of course we join our neighbors in observing the age-old customs that mark the changing seasons. At Beltaine we drive our cattle out between the rows of purifying fires into the fresh spring pastures, and we dance at Lughnasa during the celebrations in high summer when the sun gives light far into the night.

In late fall, Samhain marks the new year and the beginning of winter. Like everyone else we stay inside on Samhain Eve, when the spirits are said to leave their dwelling places in the wells, lakes, rivers, and hills to walk among the living. We make sure then to have mistletoe over the doors and windows to keep away evil.

And I have always stood in the sacred circle of women at Imbolc, the time of lambing near winter's end, for the rituals that ensure the fertility of our animals and our own good health in childbirth.

But there is an important difference between us and our neighbors. They attend the ceremonies in the Sacred Oak Grove, and we do not. We respect the Druids for their great knowledge, and we depend on them to tell us many things, but we are Christians and so are forbidden to stay in the groves at night when the bonfires blaze and the sacrifices begin.

Inside the house Moren lies as he has all day with his shoulders and head propped on folded skins. I strain in the growing darkness to watch his chest move as he breathes.

The scent of the steam rising from Aten's little iron pot, which hangs now over the inside fire, reminds me of Grenna's last days. Aten came often then to brew the herbs and stroke her friend's brow.

Others also offered help, a bit of meat from the hunt, some greens from the streamside, perhaps a fish. But through the long nights it was just the three of us, as it had been all my life. When Grenna's death came, Moren and I prepared her for her last trip, and we walked together beside her body as our friends carried her up the hill.

It seems fitting that I be alone with my father now. I pray that Aten's medicine will break the congestion in his chest. But if the dream foretells the truth and he is dying, I will be the one who sits beside him until the end. I swallow hard against the fear and push the future out of my mind.

Cryner is pressed against the bed with his long nose resting on the bedskins. He turns sad eyes to me and whines.

"Yes, boy. I know. He is ill." I pat the old dog's head and take my seat on the stool beside him.

A breeze carries the chill of coming winter through the partially open shutters. It stirs the bundles of herbs I've hung to dry from the roof poles, and the scents of thyme, peppermint, and borage mingle with the smell from Aten's medicine. I build up the fire to keep the kettle simmering. Flames dance and cast light around the room.

Cryner gives a long dog sigh and moves to his bed in the corner.

Moren stirs. His hand moves about the side of the bed as if searching, and I reach out to hold it.

"I'm here, Moren. I'll stay beside you through the night."

As I speak, he turns his head toward me and opens his eyes. I don't know if he can see me in the flickering light.

"I've waited too long." His voice is slurred from Aten's potion, but I can hear the words clearly enough. "I should have spoken."

"It is all right," I say. "It can wait until you're well."

"No." He seems to become stronger. His eyes open wider, and for a moment I'm sure that he does see me. "It is time. You must go. Grenna wanted so much to return. . . ." His voice trails off.

"Where?" I ask. "Where must I go?"

"East. To Dun Alyn." He draws a deep breath that rattles in his chest. He coughs then lies still, breathing heavily, for a time.

I wait, holding his hand.

When he opens his eyes again, he speaks in such a low voice that I have to move my ear close. "Go to Dun Alyn. Find Ryamen; she's expecting the two of us before the snows come."

He sighs and coughs but does not speak again. Soon he sleeps. I stay at his bedside throughout the night, getting up now and then to stir the fire and stretch my tired muscles.

Once I hear animals outside our wicker paddock fence. Wolves, perhaps, come down from the hills in search of chickens or lambs left unprotected. When one of them claws at the paddock gate, I move to the door, ready to take up spear and torch. The scratching stops, and I hear a quiet rustle as the pack continues down into the village.

When I cannot stay awake any longer, I rest my head on my arms and close my eyes. I listen to Moren's ragged breathing for a few moments before I fall asleep.

Near dawn a rooster rouses me. As the crowing fades, there is a deep silence that frightens me. I strain to hear any sound; perhaps the congestion is gone and he is breathing so easily I can't hear him. I wait, holding my breath, willing some small noise to come from the bedplace beside me. The quiet is broken only when another rooster in the village echoes the one that woke me.

At last a cold, dark knowledge forces itself into my mind. I raise my head and look at my father. The gray predawn light shows his eyes closed as if in sleep, his hands resting at his sides. His chest does not move.

I reach out to take his hand. The skin is cool; his fingers do not bend around mine. I pull the bedskins down and lay my head on his chest. As a child I loved to sit on his lap with my ear pressed against his tunic, listening to the strong, rhythmic beat of his heart. Now, though I press first one ear, then the other against his body, I can hear no sound.

"Moren!" The cry bursts from me, and Cryner whimpers in his sleep.

I sit clutching his stiffening hand and sobbing for a long time. At last I choke back the tears and speak the prayers that commend my father's spirit to Our Lord. As dawn sends a ray of sunlight through the crack between the shutters, I remove the pile of skins behind his head and lay his body down flat on the bedplace. I place his hands together on his chest and go out to begin the morning chores.

When Aten and Fiona arrive soon after sunup, I am tending the outside fire. They know from my face, even before I speak, that Moren is dead. Fiona hurries back to the village with the news while Aten and I prepare his body for burial.

I arrange the chain with his enameled pendant around his neck and slide his gold armbands on for the last time. The talisman of goshawk feathers, worn always on his left arm, has loosened, and I fumble with knots and thongs until it is securely retied. Then we wrap him in his best cloak and fasten it with his silver brooch.

When the villagers arrive in the afternoon to carry him up the hill, I take his sword with me. When the grave is dug and his body lowered into it, I place the elegant blade on his chest so that the gold hilt makes a cross above his heart.

Since there are no other Christians in the Vale of Enfert, I alone say the prayers of our faith. When I finish, the rest chant burial runes of the old religion. The ancient words wish him a safe journey to the Sidth, final dwelling place of the dead.

When everyone else goes down the hill, I remain for a time, trying to make sense of my loss. As dusk settles over the mountains around the vale, I say a last prayer for my father and return to the home that now is mine alone.

CHAPTER

2

The funeral gathering lasts into the night. Moren would be pleased with it. There is food enough; Jon and a friend came this morning to slaughter two of our pigs and set the roasting spit above the fire. Aten and other women of the village brought bread. The apples are ripe, and the beehives yielded a full bowl of honey. Our store of ale serves everyone several times over.

At a funeral there is always feasting and drinking to show that life goes on, and there is always the story to honor the one who has died. Our village storyteller is a woman a few years older than I; her mother and her grandfather were each village teller in their time.

When all have eaten and drunk their fill, it is time for the story. Most people settle around the fire on logs or flat rocks; a few spread skins on the ground.

The teller takes her place on a log seat where everyone can see her. She swallows a big draught of ale before she begins.

"They came at the end of the long winter."

These have been the first words of our story for as long as I can remember.

She waits for quiet and continues. "Snow had set in hard before Samhain that year and continued long past the usual time of thaws. Near Beltaine it was, and there were still patches of snow around the mud and barnyard muck.

"I saw them first." She stops for another swallow of ale and sets her bowl on the ground. "A lass I was then, out digging roots for the stew pot. The stream was running free. I was hearing the sound of it and dreaming of summer to come. Something, I still can't remember what, made me look up to the head of the valley.

"There they were, two of them, riding tall horses and leading a pack pony. I couldn't see the babe at first." She smiles at me and reaches over to pat my shoulder.

She tells how the villagers, alerted, snatched spears and staves and hurried up the path to meet the newcomers. When the signs of peace were exchanged and weapons clattered to the ground, there was plenty of interest in the strangers.

"And the babe's cry! She was near starved and so weak she could hardly wail." The teller shakes her head at the memory.

She speaks of the council that met to consider the plight of the little family. Strangers had never asked to settle in the valley before, and there was much discussion before they decided to let us live here close to the village, yet a little apart. I listen carefully while she names those who argued for and against taking in outsiders. The faces I see around the fire are all friendly enough now. No one seems to regret letting us stay.

She pauses while her ale bowl is refilled. Refreshed, she begins my favorite part of the tale. "Each year the dark-bearded ones from Eriu across the western sea had come into the vale to plunder and to carry off our young people for slaves in their cursed land. They came that year not long after Moren and Grenna had raised the buildings on this farm.

"When our lookout called the warning, we rushed up the track to meet the invaders. Moren and Grenna were busy smoothing daub onto this very house. We saw Moren drop his tools and run for the paddock. Grenna snatched Ilena up and ran into the house. We thought at first that they were escaping from the fight to come.

"But in a few moments Moren rode out from behind his barn and slowed at the door to take sword and shield from Grenna. No one here had ever heard the likes of the cry he gave then. Over and over it swelled, striking terror in the hearts of all who heard it.

"The raiders froze in their tracks partway down the slope, and we paused to watch Moren. He rode onto the path, his horse rearing and plunging as if it couldn't wait to lay tooth and hoof on the intruders. And the call! Such a swelling of the old words, and a wonder one man's voice could carry so." She stops and settles back to catch her breath and lift her ale bowl.

I can hear murmured comments from those who remember the day themselves. Moren's battle cry was a shock to the people of Enfert because they have no special calls, no warriors, and no war bands. They have always defended themselves as best they could against raiders and owe no allegiance to any chief.

I worked hard to learn that battle cry myself because Moren told me it was the call of our people. He spoke of battles turned around because the yells roused the war band to new efforts and frightened the enemy at the same time. The words, in an ancient language, are a call for victory at any cost.

The teller continues, "Moren left two of the raiders alive to carry back word that this valley was no longer safe for them. None of our young people have been carried off since."

The teller's voice is slow and solemn as she approaches the end of her story. "And so the one who came to us from the East, from somewhere he never named, made another visit to that unknown place. When he returned, he was weak and feverish.

"Ilena and Aten cared for him, but the fever burned and his breathing thickened. Before sunup this morning his spirit traveled to that other world that lies so close beside our own."

I try not to cry, but I cannot stop myself, and others

cry with me. Somehow the sharp ache inside dulls with the tears that fall. Aten holds me close.

There is rustling and standing and the noise of families gathering their things and calling to children. All say a word or two of consolation to me before they leave. Soon the path down into the village holds a line of bobbing torches, and only Aten and her family remain. She gives me a last, firm hug and joins her husband, who is helping Jon harness their horse to the cart.

Fiona appears at my side from the shadows beyond the fire. "Shall I stay with you tonight, then?"

It is tempting, but I shake my head. "I must get used to being alone, Fiona."

"If you are sure?" She waits for me to reconsider, then embraces me and hurries after her parents.

I regret refusing her offer as soon as I have the outside fire banked and the door shut behind me. I look for Cryner in his bed in the corner. He is not there. I haven't seen him all evening and supposed him to be inside, away from the commotion of the funeral gathering.

I pull the door open and call for him. "Cryner! Cryner! Come, boy. They're all gone now. Come in."

The only response is a deepening silence as night creatures grow quiet at my voice. Clouds cover the moon, and the cold wind smells of rain.

Moren brought Cryner from the East when I was a

toddler. One of my earliest memories is rolling on the ground with the pup while Moren and Grenna stood arm in arm watching us. The old dog will not survive a night out in the cold. He wheezes already and moves stiffly with joint disease.

I take a torch and thrust it into coals in the outside fire. When it blazes, I move around the yard, calling for the hound. As I enter the barn, the horses stir in their stalls. I stop to stroke Rol. Although my big sorrel stallion is a trained fighting horse, he is gentle with me and likes to nuzzle my hand, looking for apple or carrot pieces.

"I'm sorry, Rol," I tell him. "There's nothing for you tonight. Tomorrow, I promise."

There is still no sign of Cryner, and I have only one more place to look. I lift the torch high to light the path and trudge up the slope to the two graves on top of the hill. Cryner's eyes catch the torchlight before I can see the rest of him. He whimpers and thumps his tail on the soft earth as I approach. The cairn we built for Moren covers one end of his grave. The dog is sprawled across the other end with his head on his paws.

"Come, boy," I plead. "It's too cold for you out here. Come down to the warm house."

He keeps his eyes on my face. His body seems to cling more firmly to the mound of earth. In the torchlight it is hard to tell where his black-and-white coat ends and the rocky dirt begins.

"Cryner!" I speak sternly and point down the slope. "Now!"

He ignores me. I grasp his collar and pull him off the grave. He tries to climb back, but I hold him firmly. The old dog's loyalty brings tears to my eyes. Partway down the slope he gives up and stops trying to return to the grave.

Inside the house he sniffs at Moren's bedplace, then searches the room, whining and snuffling. At last he falls into his bed. His wheezes grow softer, and he finally sleeps.

When I extinguish the torch, the only light comes from the fire; I sit and stare into the coals.

Cryner moans in his dream, and I know that I too must sleep. There will be chores in the morning whether I have rested or not, and I need a clear head to decide what I should do. I am so tired that I fall asleep as soon as I lie down.

I awaken in the morning to the sound of rain spattering against the thatch. Cryner is creaking to his feet. I let him out and stand in the doorway to watch raindrops bounce off mud in the yard. The outside fire smokes as water hits live coals.

When I let Cryner back in and close the door, it is dark and dreary inside. It did not seem so when Grenna and Moren were here. My childhood was filled with song and laughter. I learned about the outside world around this table. My parents taught me about our faith and told me stories of fortresses, banquets, and battles.

I look around at the two empty bedplaces, the benches where my parents sat at mealtime, Moren's drinking horn, and the bowls stacked beside the fire. My grief is so deep that I can't even cry; I sit, silent and numb, for a long time.

The rain lessens and then stops completely. I can see light brightening around the shutters. Outside there is a sound of horse's hooves and the jingle of harness metal. Someone is moving down the track from the pass.

I collect two light spears and hurry out the door with Cryner at my heels. A large black horse stands just outside the fence. The rider sits looking over our house and barn. When he sees me, he raises his right hand slowly with no weapon in sight. I lean the spears against the side of the house and raise my right hand also. Cryner growls deep in his throat. I grasp his collar with my left hand and feel his neck hair rise and stiffen.

I wait for the traveler to speak, to state his business. He is well dressed, wearing a cloak in a bold checked pattern I haven't seen before. The first rays of the sun peer through the thinning clouds and glance off brass strips around his leather helmet. A thick black mustache covers his mouth. His eyes are hidden in the shadow cast by his helmet rim, but I can feel their relentless stare.

He sits in silence for what seems a long time. Then

he turns the horse and urges it back up the trail. Cryner growls again and tries to pull away from me. I hang on to him and watch horse and rider until they disappear over the top of the pass. The encounter leaves me uneasy, but I have other things to think about.

As I go about the morning chores, the same question turns over and over in my mind. What should I do now?

At some point as I let out the horses, clean the stalls, milk the cow, check the fish trap, and feed the flock of chickens, I realize what I must do. It is a frightening thought, but Moren's words were clear. I must travel to the East myself.

I've always known that we belonged somewhere else, that we had come, for reasons I was never told, from a home-place near the eastern sea.

In stories, we learn of people's lineage for nine generations. Even here in the Vale of Enfert folk speak of their parents, grandparents, cousins, and other relatives to identify themselves. I can't do that because I know no lineage other than daughter of Moren and Grenna.

I look like Moren: tall, with broad shoulders and full black hair that must have a plait or sturdy circlet to keep it from bushing about my head. My eyes are blue, not the pale-sky color seen here in the vale but a deep near-purple hue; Moren's, though, were gray. Grenna's eyes were not blue either, but gray-green like the sea, and I have none of her round softness or fair complexion and auburn hair.

I can name my parents, and I am proud of them; but I cannot name my parents' parents or my uncles and aunts. I don't know who else I resemble, whose voice might sound like mine, who might hold her mouth just as I do when I am thinking. And I do not know what family I belong to, what land I can call my own, what house or fortress sheltered me when I was born.

Moren meant to tell me at last, but he waited too long. The story of my lineage and the place where I belong lie in the East.

CHAPTER 3

I STOP ROL AT THE HEAD OF THE PASS. THE TREES SPREAD autumn colors across the valley. The stream murmurs and splashes beside me. A cool morning breeze carries the scent of wood smoke from rooftops below, but I am leaving before anyone is about in the village. I've said my farewells and want only to begin my journey.

I'm wearing trousers and boots, with a heavy leather vest over my tunic. Moren's war helmet fits well enough with my braided hair tucked up under it. Since I am traveling alone, it is especially important that I appear to be a man out about men's business.

I trace the gold-trimmed hilt of my sword with my finger. It rests ready to hand in its carrying case on the saddle. When I dismount, I can move it to the scabbard that hangs from my belt. My dirk, its steel blade newly sharpened, is also on my belt along with my tinderbag, sling, and leather sack full of slingstones.

Moren made a great ceremony of presenting the

sword to me a year ago. He said I was as skilled with weapons as any man he'd ever taught, and this was my reward. For a moment his presence seems real beside me, and I can almost hear him say, "Now, lass, you'll make your own destiny and submit to no one."

I brush my hand across my face and rub the tears on my trousers.

I should wait to tell Jon goodbye. He will be disappointed to arrive and find me gone, but we've said all there is to say these past few days. We agreed that he would move into the house and care for the animals and tend the fields until I come back.

If I come back.

We've talked often since the funeral. Jon cannot understand my desire to go east. There is a life for me here and a place beside him. I explained that my feelings for him were those for a brother. At last he stopped trying to change my mind. I'm sure he will marry someone else soon.

Something moves in our yard. Cryner has come out to look for me.

The tears flow hard now. I know I will not see the old dog again. I fed him meat for breakfast and hugged him close. The urge to turn Rol back down the trail is strong. I could carry my things inside and put the spears by the door, my sword in its spot near my bedplace, and the valuables back into the hole beneath the loose stone.

I would say to Jon, "I've changed my mind." I know how the smile would brighten his face.

Rol tosses his head and snorts. I turn him away from the valley and down the far side of the pass. How hard it must have been for Grenna to force her tired horse up this steep path with me weak and crying in her arms! Why did they undertake a journey so soon after my birth? And why did they leave their home to brave the worst winter weather in anyone's memory? I hope to find answers to my questions at Dun Alyn.

We halt for a few minutes' rest at the bottom of the slope. The wide trail that crosses northern Britain stretches as far as I can see in either direction. Westward lies the Oak Grove.

Like everyone else in Enfert I looked forward to Midsummer's Day. As soon as it was light, all of us would make the two-hour trip to the clearing beside the Sacred Grove. Through the morning we would visit with people from other valleys, trade livestock, buy pottery or ironware, and share the food we'd brought with us.

In the afternoon we would listen to Gersmal, who has been a Druid in this area for as long as I can remember, tell news from all over Britain and even stories from faraway places like Rome and Gaul.

The Druids are the wisest and best-educated men and women in Britain. They alone know the ancient law code. They can foretell the future from the path of a wild hare and read omens in the flights of birds. Druids are trained to detect shapeshifters and determine if their intentions are for good or evil.

It is the Druids who know the calendar for the year. Gersmal would speak at length about weather predictions and seasonal movements of the animals we hunt. He would tell us which days are safe for travel, when to plant our crops, and what times are favorable for hunting.

Disputes over land, cattle, or other matters would come before him for judgment. Families or whole villages might ask for spells of protection from enemies or for ways to counter a curse laid against them.

But as the sun lowered in the west, Moren would urge Grenna and me toward our horses. The others would stay for the bonfires, the rituals of the stagman, and finally the sacrifices. We would be back in the Vale of Enfert by nightfall. The rest would fall asleep under the great trees and leave for home at dawn.

I learned what happened in those long evenings in the darkening Oak Grove from my friends. I had nightmares for weeks after some of the stories. When I asked Moren about the sacrifices, he looked grim and shook his head before he answered.

"It is the old way, lass. A plan to rid the tribe of someone who won't follow the customs or to dispose of prisoners taken in battle."

"But what about the child?" I asked. "Jon said they sacrificed a child."

He hesitated a long time before he answered. "I don't know. Perhaps it was crippled, unable to grow up properly, or unusual in some other way." He was silent again for a time. At last he said, "Most places have stopped human sacrifice. Even before monks came with the new religion, the worst of the old customs had begun to die out."

"Then," I asked, "is Gersmal the only Druid who kills people in the Oak Groves?"

"No," he said. "There are others." He walked away then and refused to discuss it any further.

I turn Rol to the east. We travel steadily all morning, and stop at noon in a clearing where ashes mark the fires of old camps. I recognize the place from a hunting trip two years ago.

Moren and I had ranged far into the forest, sometimes on paths no wider than our horses, in search of game. We got back to the main trail by nightfall, but darkness trapped us here a half-day's ride from home. Moren cut the ritual portion from the deer I'd brought down with my spear and burned it as an offering of thanks for success in the hunt. Then we cooked some of the meat for ourselves and Cryner. It was the old hound's last trip with us.

I unharness Rol so he can graze in comfort. I carry very little with me. Food for myself and oats for Rol are tied on top of my pack along with my cloak. The pack holds a clean tunic and undergarments, slippers, the blue dress from the last of Grenna's weaving, and an elegant girdle Moren brought me last summer. I have my bracelets and gold circlet along with Grenna's bronze mirror and her finest bone comb.

The heaviest things in the bundle are the bag of coins and the gold torc. I found both yesterday in the safe hole beneath a loose floor stone in our house. I pulled the bag of coins out to take with me. Without Moren's armbands and pendant, the hollow should have been empty, but I caught sight of leather far back in the space. I tugged it out and unwrapped layers of old skins.

An afternoon sunbeam slanting through the window caught the heavy neckpiece as I laid it on the table. I stared at it, amazed; I had never seen so much gold. The circlet for my hair is a thin gold band with enameled circles decorating the ends, and my bracelets are lightweight twists of thin gold wire. Even Moren's pendant does not hold as much gold as the torc.

It is formed of eight ropes of gold twisted together. Each rope is made up of eight gold wires wrapped around each other. The whole is bent into a circular shape with large terminals, elaborately carved, marking the ends. I can feel its weight as I lift my pack to the ground. I try to imagine how it would feel around my neck.

I remove the case of casting spears, the two long war spears, my round shield, and the waterskin. Finally I take off the saddle and unfasten the bridle bit. It is a lot of work, but Rol must rest and eat if we are to continue traveling all day.

After he drinks from the small stream that runs beside the clearing, I let him crop grass while I sit with my back against a tree to eat bread and dried meat. I close my eyes and am almost asleep when a sound startles me. Rol has stopped grazing and stands with his ears forward. He faces the way we've come. I listen intently for a time but don't hear anything else.

Rol relaxes and goes back to eating. Now there are only bird and insect noises, but I don't close my eyes again.

When he is rested, we set out under a warm afternoon sun. The trail is joined from time to time by tracks that lead off into the forest, and it widens as we travel.

I don't see anyone else until late afternoon. My first warning that there are other people around is a sound of metal clashing. At first it is so faint that I am not sure what it is. As I come closer, I recognize the clang of weapons. I stop Rol and pull a casting spear from the holder behind me. I drop the reins so I can loosen my sword with my other hand. At that moment the forest is rent by an unearthly sound.

It is the scream of a fighting stallion, and it echoes again and again around us. Rol, without my firm hand on the rein, leaps forward toward the cries. By the time I have him under control, we have burst out of cover into a large clearing.

A magnificent gray stallion rears and flails his hooves over the heads of several short, dark-bearded men. Their rough clothing and short spears mark them as slave traders like those who raided Enfert every year until Moren arrived.

The big horse is turning and leaping with his iron-shod front feet beating down at them. Behind the stallion a man lies on the ground without moving. Sunlight sparkles on the gold hilt of a long sword beside him.

Rol jerks his head against the bit and tries to join the fight. Two of the men hear him and turn toward us. The gray stallion strikes at their backs and both fall. The rest glance toward Rol and then back to the gray. It rears higher and cries again. I cannot hold Rol, and he too rears and trumpets. I pull him down and regain control. He stands, quivering and snorting but obedient to my stern commands.

One of the men still standing says something I don't understand. I raise my spear and let Rol move toward them. They hasten out of the clearing, dragging their wounded with them.

I calm Rol and dismount. The gray horse is quieter now. He paces a wide half-circle in front of the fallen man. I walk slowly and speak to the stallion. He moves constantly to keep between me and his master, and I know that even if I could grasp his reins, I would not be able to hold him.

The man on the ground stirs and moans.

"Sir," I call. "Sir, I can help you if your horse will allow it."

I see his lips move, but I can't hear what he says.

"Your horse won't let me near," I say.

He tries to raise himself but falls back. The horse turns and nuzzles him. I move closer, and the horse whirls to head me off.

The man manages to speak. "Bork . . . Bork . . . All right. It's all right now."

The horse steps back a few paces. I advance carefully, watching those big front hooves.

"He's all right now. He heard me."

"A fighter, that one," I say.

"Aye." His voice is stronger, but he still lies flat on the rocky ground. "Are they gone, lad?"

It sounds strange, but I'm glad to be taken for a male. "Gone. For good, I'd guess. I'll get water for you." Rol has remained where I left him. I stroke his neck for a minute to reassure him before I carry my waterskin to the injured man.

He sits with my help and takes the container in his hands. I study him while he drinks. Auburn hair curls around his leather war helmet and tangles into a short auburn beard. His face under the grime and streaks of blood is ruddy with the constant sunburn of the truly fair-skinned. The eye I can see is gray-green; the other has already swollen shut. I'd guess him to be from the South, of a lineage like Grenna's.

The blood comes from an abrasion on his forehead.

It looks like the mark of a slingstone. He fingers it cautiously.

I ask, "Do you feel well enough to travel?"

"Aye. Soon. I'm just dizzy from the blow." He reaches up slowly and removes his helmet. "Thank you for coming to my aid." His speech is familiar with the words and cadences I learned from Moren and Grenna.

"My horse decided for me."

"This trail is a dangerous place for a lad alone. You are alone?"

I hesitate. He looks safe enough. His fine clothes and the horse's well-made harness suggest he would have no interest in my belongings.

He sees my reluctance to answer. "I'm sorry. That is not a courteous question. What I mean is, will you make camp with me tonight? Two of us will be safer than one."

The thought of raiders in the area convinces me. "I'd be glad of company."

"I am Durant, liege to Arthur. I travel here in the North on his business." He waits for my response.

"I'm . . ." I stop. He's going to think I'm slow-witted if I must ponder every answer, but I hadn't thought of a name. Ilena is certainly not a man's name. "Ilun," I finally manage to say. "Of the Vale of Enfert."

"Let's move on, Ilun. I doubt they'll be back"—he glances toward the trail the raiders have taken—"but it's time to stop for the night, and I don't fancy this place." He moves to gain his feet, and I reach out to help him. I grasp his forearm and feel the bulging muscles of a practiced swordsman. He is taller than I, as tall as Moren.

Bork eyes me with some distrust, but he stands still enough while I help his master into the saddle and slip his sword into its case. Durant grasps the pommel and sways from side to side as Bork walks out of the clearing.

I watch the forest around us closely, looking for any break in the trees that might signal a path into a sheltered spot. The red evening sun is disappearing by the time we locate a suitable place. Branches scrape at my trousers as I lead the way through thick evergreens. I can hear a stream nearby, and a cliff along one side gives shelter.

Darkness has almost overtaken this clearing. There is a rich scent of mud and greenery. Even the sounds of birds and insects seem muffled here. The heavy foliage and solid cliffs give the tiny space a welcome feeling of safety.

"Rest," I say. "I'll water the horses and see to the fire." Durant dismounts without speaking. His knees buckle, and he holds on to the saddle. I hurry to help him. He is able to walk with my support, and I leave him sitting on a flat rock against the cliff.

Bork looks back as I lead him toward the sound of running water, but Durant calls out in a shaky voice, "Go on, boy. It's all right. Go." The big gray snorts and follows alongside Rol.

Durant seems stronger after he has rested and eaten. I move his pack to a flat space between the cliff and the small fire I've built. I sweep sticks and debris away and make a bed with pine boughs and his saddlecloth. He lowers himself carefully and adjusts the pack for a pillow. He is asleep by the time I've finished feeding the horses.

I pull off my helmet and shake my hair loose. I'm not sure what to do about my disguise as a young man. Durant is courteous and speaks like a man of honor; I think I can trust him.

I leave my helmet and leather vest by the fire when I go to the stream to wash. While I'm there, I make a poultice of mud and leaves and carry it back to Durant. He seems to be sleeping soundly, but he stirs and opens his good eye when I put the cold pack against his swollen forehead.

He looks puzzled. The eye opens wider, and he sits up. The poultice tumbles into his lap. "Ilun? Ilun of the Vale of Enfert?" He stares at my unbound hair and at my bodice where my wet tunic clings to my body.

I back away from him and hope the firelight doesn't reveal the flush I feel burn across my face.

"Not a lad at all, it seems." I can hear the amusement in his voice. I remember the laughter of boys at home when they enticed one of the girls off to a hidden place. My sword and spears are across the fire. Even my dirk is there where I dropped it with my vest and helmet.

He follows my glance, and a frown crosses his face for a moment. "What is your name, lass?"

I do not answer. I don't want to give even that to a strange man. I move farther away.

He reaches out and grasps my wrist with a firm hold, but his voice is gentle. "I'm sorry I laughed. You surprised me. Do I look so frightening to you? Do you really think I would harm you?"

"Some men say it is not harm but only what is natural."

"I well know what some men say and do. I am not a man who forces women. I am pledged to Arthur's table. It is our oath to protect women from the danger you fear."

"I have heard that from the bards," I admit. "I did not know if it was true."

He speaks slowly as if to make sure I understand. "It is true, lass. If you do not wish to tell me your name, I'll call you Ilun. I want nothing from you that's not freely given."

Perhaps it is his manner or my need for a friend, or maybe it's something I do not understand in this isolated spot, but I believe him. His grip on my wrist has relaxed. I could pull away from him, but I find I draw comfort from his rough palm against my skin.

"I'm called Ilena. I apologize for giving you the wrong name, but my father taught me always to travel as a man."

He nods carefully. He finds the cold pack with his

free hand and holds it against the swelling. "That is good advice indeed. Still, it is not safe for a woman to travel alone in any costume. How did your father let you leave without an escort?"

I take a deep breath. For most of the day I've put Moren's death into a corner of my mind. Speaking about it will bring back the pain. "He is dead." I can say no more and look down to hide my sudden tears.

He says, "I'm sorry. Have you no one? Your mother? A brother?"

I shake my head. His hand still rests on my arm. The gentle pressure sends unfamiliar sensations through my body. I move casually as if to ease my muscles with a new position and break the contact between us. My skin tingles where his hand has been.

We are both silent for a time. The fire crackles beside us, and I can hear faint night noises in the surrounding forest. Something moves beyond the thick circle of trees in the direction of the stream—an animal looking for water or for its dinner. We listen till it passes.

I remember Cryner looking for me this morning and my comfortable bedplace in the snug house I've left behind.

Durant's voice brings me back to the clearing. "You seem far away, Ilena."

"I was thinking of my home."

"Why have you left so late in the season? And where do you travel?"

"I go to relatives in the East," I say. "I hope to move ahead of the snows."

"You shouldn't travel alone."

I try to sound courageous. "I must go to Dun Alyn."

"Dun Alyn, is it?" He moves his head away from the cliff and winces. "I need to lie down. Let us talk more of this tomorrow."

We are not disturbed through the night. I wake to a cold rain that has put out the fire. Durant seems rested, though the swelling is worse. I convince him to sit and eat while I saddle our horses.

As I spread the saddlecloth over Rol's back, I notice Durant lowering his head and tracing the sign of a cross over his bread. His lips move, though I can't hear what he says. He looks up to see me watching him.

"I am a Christian," he says. "It is thus that we thank Our Lord for his gifts of food and health."

"I know," I say. "I do the same at morning bread, but all the others in our valley follow the Druids. I am surprised to see another Christian."

"And I did not expect to find one of my faith in this area," he says. "Do the monks visit the Vale of Enfert?"

"Aye, a few," I answer. "Our home has been a convenient stop for those who travel from the western isles, and my parents always gave them a warm welcome."

"Have you encountered hostility for your faith?"

"No, but my father always spoke of the Druids with respect, though we did not attend the sacrifices."

"That was sensible. The Druids have been our religious leaders and legal experts for hundreds of years." He pulls Bork close to a large stone so that he can mount more easily.

I see that Durant is in pain as he settles into the saddle, and I say, "You need rest."

"We'll be at Dun Dreug by noon. I can rest there."

"We?"

We are both mounted now. He leads the way out of the clearing, and the horses settle into a steady jog. The track is wide enough for us to ride side by side.

I repeat my question. "We? I do not plan to visit Dun Dreug."

"You cannot wander about unescorted."

He seems to have forgotten that I was unescorted when I saved him yesterday, but I say only, "I ride beyond Dun Dreug."

"Yes, Dun Alyn is two days farther east. I would like to see you safely there. But first I must wait for word from Arthur at Dun Dreug. Where I go next depends on the latest news of Saxon movements."

"And I must go on as I have planned."

The discussion is cut short as we hear horses approach. Durant guides Bork in front of Rol, and we ride forward slowly, single file. I shift the reins to my left hand, ready to seize a weapon or raise my hand in greeting. Durant loosens his sword in its holder before he lifts his arm in the sign of peace.

There are three men and one woman in the party

that rides toward us. They too have slowed and prepared for whatever greeting is appropriate. We pass with right hands high and empty, our eyes on one another's weapons.

The man in front is short and heavy. His beard bushes down over his heavy vest, and blue streaks mark his forehead under an iron helmet. The woman behind him is older than I, with a thick braid of black hair falling below her helmet. She wears leather armor and trousers. Tattoos decorate her cheeks and forehead. Her dark eyes stare into mine. We nod slightly to each other as her gray-and-white dappled mare passes close to Rol. The two following are also in leather armor with war helmets, and both bear blue markings on their faces.

After they pass, Durant falls back beside me and whispers, "Look back in case they stop. I can't see well with this eye."

I loosen my grip on the reins so Rol can find his own way and turn in the saddle. The last man in the party is watching us. He waves with his right hand, and I do the same. We stare at each other until Durant and I round a bend that blocks our view.

"Are those of the painted people?" I ask.

"Yes. Many in this area wear some decoration, but only the painted people from beyond Red Mountain still tattoo their faces."

"Are they a danger to us?"

"It is hard to know. Their clans, like ours, form new

alliances constantly. A few of the painted ones have pledged to join with Arthur in his fight against the Saxon invaders, but most band together to oppose him. My task here in the North is to bring everyone who will join Arthur into a firm alliance. As the Saxons push farther and farther north, Britons must band together, or we will all be conquered."

I know well that Moren believed that. He questioned any traveler into the valley about news of Arthur and the spread of Saxon power. I ask, "Does Dun Alyn follow Arthur?"

"We don't know," he says. "What word do you have from your people there?"

"My father returned from Dun Alyn two weeks ago, but he was too ill to talk about his trip." I hope he doesn't ask the names of my people in the East. It is a shameful thing to be unable to recite one's lineage.

Whenever I asked Moren or Grenna about my birthplace or about our relatives, they would answer, "In time, Ilena. In time. There is no need for you to know now."

I ride on in silence. There are too many questions in my mind, and each one leads to another more confusing.

Near noon we break out of forest cover onto the bank of a lake. I can see across it, but the length stretches out of sight. Rain has ceased, although gray clouds mask the sun. We stop to water the horses and rest. Durant is shaky when he dismounts. He moves cautiously to sit on a fallen tree and slumps over with his head down while I loosen the horses' bits so they can graze.

I take two bannocks and a strip of dried meat from my pack. I tear the meat in two and offer a piece to him along with one of the loaves. He accepts them with a weak nod but doesn't begin to eat. I fill our waterskins and carry his to him.

"Thank you, Ilena." He drinks and takes a bite of the bread. "I felt well enough when we started this morning, but my head swims now."

I reach over to touch the wound. His forehead is hot, and the swelling seems worse than it was this morning. "You need rest and a proper poultice for this," I say. "How much farther to Dun Dreug?"

"Not far. It's at the end of this lake. Let's keep going. I can manage." He scowls at the meat, then takes a small bite.

When we move on, I hold Rol to a walk, hoping the smooth gait will be easier for Durant. Bork is impatient but finally settles down to match Rol's pace. The wide track near the water's edge is easy, and my mind wanders while Rol ambles along.

I've no desire to detour from my own journey, but it is afternoon already. Stopping for the night with hope of a bed and hot food is tempting. And I might learn something about Dun Alyn.

CHAPTER 4

DUN DREUG IS VISIBLE LONG BEFORE WE REACH IT. THE walls of earth and stone stand on a ridgetop above the lake. Durant turns us onto a well-traveled trail that winds its way up to the summit. There we follow a high road to the gates. The lake lies gray and calm far below. Gulls swoop and call over the water, and there is a wide view over the hills and valleys in all directions.

The earthen defenses that ring the outside of the complex would surround the entire Vale of Enfert. I keep a proper appearance with my back straight and my head high as we approach. We are challenged at the mouth of the first ring.

"Who goes, and what is your business?"

"Durant of Hadel, envoy from Arthur. My business is with Perr."

"And your companion?"

"Ilena of Enfert in the West. She travels with me."

The gatekeepers, youths about my age, not yet

bearded, step back to let us pass. There is no one at the opening to the second earthen ring, but a small troop of warriors stands around tall wooden gates in the inner stone wall. One of them calls to us.

"Ho! Durant, is that you? And who is with you?"

"Aye, Bracios, what's left of me after a too-well-aimed slingstone. The lady Ilena travels under my protection."

I nod in what I hope is a ladylike greeting. Under his protection, indeed! And yet it saves a lot of trouble. There will be no advances, no questions I don't want to deal with.

The gates creak open, and we ride into Dun Dreug. I have heard stories of fortresses. The descriptions filled stanzas of the bards' songs, and Grenna and Moren often told of holdings they had known. Still, I am unprepared for the sheer size of the compound or for the commotion before me.

There are structures everywhere I look. A round building like the houses at home but much larger stands farthest from the gate. It must be the Great Hall. People swarm in and out of doors like ants going about their business on a hot summer day. Hounds and children chase each other around buildings and across the grounds.

We head directly to the Great Hall. The man who stands before its door wears wide gold armbands, and his sword hilt shines above an ornate scabbard.

"Elban, Chief Perr's good friend and doorkeeper," Durant says as we approach.

Elban steps forward to greet us. "Welcome, Durant of Hadel. Chief Perr has been told of your arrival."

He has hardly finished speaking when a man hurries through the wide door behind him. "Durant! Blessings on the feet that brought you. We've been expecting you for days."

Durant slides down from Bork's back. I can see the effort he makes to stay upright. His face is pale around the ugly swelling, and his knuckles are white where he clutches a saddle strap. He smiles, however, and speaks in a hearty voice. "Blessing on this house, Perr. And a welcome sight you are."

Perr of Dun Dreug is short and nearly as broad as he is high. His beard and hair are brown streaked with gray. Bright blue eyes are alert under heavy brown eyebrows. His hair is held in a curious circlet of gold wire that ends in flat gold animal heads pressed against his temples. He wears leather trousers and a loose vest over a finely woven tunic. A gold pendant inlaid with red and blue enamel hangs tangled in brown chest hair at the tunic's opening.

He turns to me with a nod. "And welcome to your companion."

"The lady Ilena." Durant makes no further explanation for me.

"A blessing on this house and all who live here, Chief Perr." I move to dismount, and Elban springs to Rol's side.

"My arm, lady."

"Thank you." I hardly need help getting off my horse, but I lay my hand on the thick brown forearm he offers.

"I need rest, Perr, and perhaps a poultice for this eye," Durant says. "Then we can talk."

"My wife, Faren, is skilled with wounds; she'll treat it for you. I'll show you to your sleeping space." Perr looks toward me.

I flush at the unspoken question that hangs in the air.

"The lady Ilena would like the women's quarters." Durant smiles at me.

Boys have appeared to take the horses. I reach to lift down my pack, but Elban moves in front of me. "I'll get that, lady." He slings my pack on his shoulder and takes my sword and shield from the harness.

I nod to Chief Perr and Durant and follow my guide toward a building off to the side of the Great Hall. He carries my shield and pack together on his shoulder with one hand and holds my sword in the other so he can study the hilt.

"Gola, Gola! Hurry up!" When a woman a little older than I appears, Elban continues. "This is the lady Ilena. She rode in with Arthur's envoy. Find her fitting quarters."

He hands my pack over to her and offers sword and shield to me. "A fine sword this, lady. Made by Master Trelawn, I'd wager."

"I don't know. It was a gift, and I treasure it highly."

"That you should. Gola will tell you when it is time to gather in the Great Hall for dinner." His nod to me is almost a bow.

Gola wears her full auburn hair loose, and it falls from a simple silver circlet. She has a bronze-and-silver brooch at the shoulder of her brown dress. She leads me across a dim room with a low fire in the center hearth and into a fine sleeping room with walls taller than I. There is a deerskin to drop over the entrance for privacy and a window onto the courtyard.

She closes the shutters. "It blows cold from the north, lady. We fear snow early this year."

Bad news, that, for me. I've heard enough of Moren's trips to know that there are mountain passes yet to cross before I reach Dun Alyn. If there is a chance of snow, I must move on quickly.

"The servants are busy in the kitchen," Gola says. "I'll bring you a basin of water."

"Thank you," I say. "That will be welcome." I open my pack and shake out the blue gown and the girdle. I spread them over one end of the long bedplace and lay my circlet and bracelets with them.

Gola returns with a basin of steaming water and a towel. "I'll return for this when you've finished. Most of the ladies are at chariot races beyond the northern wall. You have time to rest before they return."

The hot water feels good. I wash away the grime and horse smell and pull on a clean undershift. There is still no one in the building but me, and the bed is inviting. It feels good to stretch out.

When I awaken I hear voices, but they seem to be fading. Someone has removed the basin and towel. I push the doorskin aside and peer out into the rest of the house; two women are moving toward the front entrance. They are too engrossed in their conversation to notice me, but I get a good view of a gold pendant, bracelets, and gleaming circlets.

There's a harp playing in the distance, and I smell roasted meat. I find Grenna's comb and attack the tangles in my hair.

"Lady Ilena." Gola bustles in. "You've had a long rest. Can I help you get ready?" She takes the comb from my hand and points to the bed. "Sit."

I obey and let her work. She picks up the gold circlet. "Lovely," she says when it's adjusted to her satisfaction.

I stand to pull on the blue gown and find her holding it ready. I can barely remember Grenna helping me dress when I was a child, and I've certainly had no one combing and holding and smoothing for me since. Being taken for a lady is an interesting experience. Gola exclaims over the fine needlework on the girdle and hands me my bracelets.

"Is the mirror there in my pack?" I ask.

She rummages around for a moment and pulls it out with one hand. With the other she draws forth the gold torc. "Oh, lady. This is priceless!" She reaches out and clasps it around my neck, then hands me the mirror.

The torc is heavy against my neck, but the feeling is not unpleasant. I can see the metal gleaming in the smooth bronze mirror. It calls attention to my face and to the thin circlet that holds my hair. I have no idea whether I should wear it or not, but Gola thinks I am appropriately adorned for the Great Hall.

"Oh, Lady Ilena, you'll be the envy of every woman there."

I'm not sure if that is my goal, but they think I'm a noblewoman of some sort, so I should try to play the part. I take my light slippers from the pack and pull them on.

"I'll walk with you to the Great Hall," Gola offers.

The sentries greet me when we arrive. They have taken Elban's place at the entrance. The position of doorkeeper is important and a great honor. If no strangers are anticipated, Elban will eat at Perr's table. The sentries will call him if they need help deciding whether someone should enter the hall.

"Lady Ilena. Chief Perr and his wife wait for you at the head table."

Inside the hall I stand for several minutes adjusting my eyes to the dim, smoky room. In truth it is more than the change in light that makes me pause. The noise of dozens of people talking, calling between tables, laughing, and, at one table near the front, clapping their hands overwhelms me. Harp music fills any spaces in the din.

I've never dreamed of so many people in one place. Most sit on benches at long tables that fill the room. Servants run about with baskets of bread and fruits. Women hurry to a huge cauldron at one side to refill flagons for those at their tables. Torches sputter above it all, adding light to fading twilight from the windows and smoke to the scent of meats and human bodies.

I realize I've been standing there for too long when the hall grows quiet and people turn to stare at me. Gola touches my arm and points across the room to a long table raised on a platform. Chief Perr sits in the center; a tall blond-haired woman stands at his side. She is beckoning to me and pointing to an empty seat beside her.

"I'll find you after dinner," Gola says. She moves off into the crowd.

I remember to raise my chin and square my shoulders before I start across the hall. It is important to look confident whether I feel so or not. Moren reminded me often that people keep their first impressions for a long time. As I move along an aisle that stretches between tables to the platform, I hear whispers.

"Rode in with Durant."

"His woman?"

". . . somewhere in the West."

"See that torc?"

". . . staying in the women's quarters."

By the time I reach the head table and take the seat beside Chief Perr's wife, conversation has resumed at full volume. I can hardly hear her words. "Welcome to Dun Dreug. I am Faren. Durant tells me you are from the West?"

It is rude to ask direct questions of a guest, but I can tell that she hopes for information. I smile and try to speak without admitting that I have no noble lineage to report. "From the Vale of Enfert, lady. It is near the western sea."

"And your father is chief of Enfert?"

"My father is dead."

"I'm sorry to hear that." She touches the sleeve of my dress. "This is lovely weaving. The color suits you."

I start to acknowledge the compliment, but we are interrupted by a serving boy with a plank of meats from the carving table. After two days of dried venison and stale bread, the hot food is welcome. I pull my dirk from its holder in my girdle and spear a large piece of beef. There are also pork and several small birds still on a spit. I pull one of the birds onto my trencher.

Gola appears at my shoulder with a flagon of ale.

"Thank you," I say. "I didn't see where you went when we came in."

"I am sitting there." She points back into shadows

near the door. "My husband and I ride with Perr's war band."

Conversation stops at table after table as servants progress through the hall with the food. I wish Fiona and Jon could be here. We used to play at heroes' banquets when we were small. Occasionally a bard would venture into the Vale of Enfert looking for dinner and a bed in exchange for his stories and fresh news. For days afterward we would act out the stories we had heard of heroes and banquets.

My old friends would be surprised to see me at the head table in this great hall wearing a gold torc and talking with a chief and his wife.

As the music strengthens, Faren whispers, "A new bard. He arrived today."

Chief Perr leans past his wife and speaks to me. "He brings news of fortresses in the East. Durant will want to know what he tells us."

The bard brings his music to a close and stands to speak. First he thanks Perr and his wife for their hospitality. He talks for a while of Arthur and of new Saxon invasions in the South, then strikes several strong chords and announces a title:

"The Story of Cara and Miquain."

Some in the hall turn on their benches to see better. Others hurry to get fresh ale before the music starts again. The bard moves his stool toward the center of the platform and waits for silence. I can see him well now; his sharp-nosed profile is directly in front of me. His rusty brown hair hangs in unruly locks around his face as he bends over his instrument.

When the hall is quiet, he begins speaking over soft chords from the harp. "I have just come from my first visit to Dun Alyn. All there are still in mourning for the ladies of the fortress."

Perr drops his dirk on the table and stands to lean toward the bard. "By the gods, man, what do you mean?"

"They were killed in battle some thirty days ago."

"Both of them?"

"Aye," the bard answers.

"And Belert?" Perr asks.

"He lives. Listen, and I will sing the story as I learned it at Dun Alyn."

I stop eating. The meat that seemed so welcome a few minutes ago sits like a stone in my belly. I had hoped for news of Dun Alyn, but I didn't expect anything this dreadful. I lean forward to be sure I can hear it all. The rest of the hall is quiet and every eye is fixed on the bard. Perr sits down and pushes his trencher away.

The bard strums one loud chord, then holds the harp silent while he speaks. "In the days before Vortigern, before Saxons menaced our southern shore, the mighty Chief Fergus with his lady, Gwlech, led Dun Alyn. This is the story of their daughter, Cara, and her daughter, Miquain."

He plays a few notes of a melody and then begins to sing in a clear, strong voice:

Fairer than snow on the slopes of Red Mountain
Cara, the daughter of Gwlech and Fergus.
Lighter than breezes her steps in the hall
When the company gathered at twilight.
Bright was her face, brighter than starlight
Shining in blackness at midnight.
Higher than clouds was her beauty
Above the daughters of chiefs around her.
Hair that glistened like the raven's wing,
Skin of white like wave tops in a winter storm,
Cheeks blushed red as any scarlet berry in the sun.
Her eyes gray as trout pools on a cloudy day.
Long the suitors clamored
At the gates of Dun Alyn.

Cara, maiden of the North,
Sung for her beauty
From the day that she could walk,
Took sword and lance into battle,
Led Dun Alyn's warriors.
Stood beside her father
When war bands from the islands
Landed ships beneath the cliff
Where Dun Alyn towers high above the strand.

Fierce she battled
Till her foes were slain around her.

Their bodies on the ground
Piled like apples in the harvest,
Their heads upon the ramparts
Pierced like meats above the fire
Spoke to all who saw
Of the mighty battle wrought by Cara,
Daughter of Gwlech and of Fergus.
She stood beside her father on the shore.
She stood beside her father at the gates.
And stood beside her father on his deathbed.
Wounded hard by a raider's lance,
The mighty Fergus was no more.

Cara, treasure of her mother's line,
Sought among her suitors
For a man to rule beside her
Until Belert came to woo her.
Long the feasts and sweet the songs,
For a month the banquet lasted.
Cara rode with Belert,
Side by side they urged
Their chariots against the foe.

Dun Alyn prospered,
Held its walls secure
Against raiders from the sea
And painted ones around them.
Cara brought to childbed

With the fair Miquain.
Raised her daughter as a warrior
Like to herself she raised her
Till the two rode forth together,
Black hair streaming in the wind.
Brave as her father, skilled as her mother,
Miquain stood fair among the women
Who graced the northern halls.

The bard stills the harp strings and reaches for his drink. People shift around on the benches and make quiet comments to one another. When the hall falls silent, the musician strums a few chords and speaks above them. "It was a dark night soon after Lughnasa when raiders sailed down the coast and beached their boats below Dun Alyn. They waited unseen, silent, while the gates opened for the day, and they watched as Belert and his men rode out to hunt."

He plays a strain of melody and then begins to sing again:

War bands from afar,
Painted ones and foreigners
From across the eastern water
Struck when Dun Alyn was at its weakest,
Belert with his war band,
Heroes bound to die before surrender,
Hunting in the forest.

Women and youth left behind
To guard the fortress.

Loud the horn that signaled danger.
Swift, Miquain's response.
With her mother close behind
Sent her chariot out the gate
To engage the foe in battle.
Red the stream that runs beside Dun Alyn,
Red with blood of the attackers,
Red with blood of Dun Alyn's pride.

Belert far beyond the fortress
Heard the noise of battle horns,
Spurred his horse toward home.
Heard the noise of clashing weapons.
Led his men till horses stumbled
From the effort of the charge.
Came at last to see invaders at the gate.
Cara and Miquain, treasures of his life,
Dead beside the others
At the stream below the gate.
He worked a terrible vengeance,
Left no raider alive to reach
The boats upturned along the beach.

Loud the wails, long the mourning
For Dun Alyn's ladies, flowers of the North.
Belert lost in grief haunts Dun Alyn's walls.
Looking seaward now and landward then.
Looking far beyond the land of mortals,

Wishing only that he'd joined them
In their journey to the Sidth.

Gloom hangs heavy on Dun Alyn's hill.
Sing the death of Cara.
Sing the death of Miquain.
Lament with Belert, chief of Dun Alyn.

The bard's head lowers closer and closer to his harp until his forehead rests against the frame on the last words. The final chord hangs for a time in the silent room, then dies away as hushed talking resumes.

CHAPTER 5

THE STORY MAKES ME WEEP. I TRY TO STOP THE TEARS that overflow and streak my cheeks.

"Are you well, Ilena?" The chief's wife lays a gentle hand on my arm. "Do you have ties to Dun Alyn?"

"Yes. I have kin there," I say. At least I think that's true.

The bard strums quietly as the hall continues to buzz with the news. At last he plays a loud chord to get attention and starts the familiar story of the first Saxons in the South and the alliances that gave them territory.

I let my mind wander back to the story of Cara and Miquain. Moren must have arrived at Dun Alyn soon after the battle. Would the deaths have had special meaning to him?

A movement in the center of the hall catches my eye. A man is walking between tables. There is something familiar about him. The set of his shoulders, perhaps. He turns, and I see a full black mustache and heavy brows. He looks like the traveler who rode into the Vale of Enfert the morning after Moren's funeral. I peer through the haze in the hall, but I cannot see clearly enough to know if it is the same man.

The music stops, and Perr rises to offer one last salute—to Arthur and his latest victory against the Saxons. Most remain standing after the toast and begin the bustle of leavetaking, gathering up dirks, bidding table-mates good evening, making a courteous comment to Perr or his wife.

I move away from the head table to find Gola at my side. "Can I do anything for you, lady?"

"Thank you, Gola. I would like to visit Durant. Can you show me where he is?"

"Let me ask Elban." She hurries away in search of Perr's doorkeeper.

"We've tucked him here in the men's hall." Elban leads me to a building behind the Great Hall. It is much like the women's quarters, with a fire in the center and sleeping spaces partitioned off around the sides. Most doorskins are pulled aside to let heat into the cubicles. Elban points to a door along the wall to the left of the entry. Its entrance skin is closed.

"Durant. Durant, are you there?" I call quietly, so as not to wake him if he sleeps.

"Ilena. Pull the doorskin aside and come in. Forgive me for not getting up."

I jerk the large deer hide to one side and enter.

Durant is propped against bedskins on a wide sleeping bench. His head is wrapped in a large bandage that covers his swollen eye. The window has been closed against the evening cold, and a fire is crackling in a three-legged brazier.

His greeting is unexpectedly sharp. "Stand over there. By the fire."

I step obediently into the light cast by the flames.

He turns his head in order to see me clearly with his good eye. "By the gods. No wonder!"

I wait, not sure what reply to make to that.

"Two visiting chiefs already. Asking about you. One for himself and another for his son." He sounds more amused than irritated. "And do you wish marriage to an old man or a young?"

"I do not wish marriage at all," I say. "And why do you think I do?"

"I hadn't thought about it. The two who've come were in a hurry to be here before others. Now that I see you out of leather armor and helmet I know why."

I move away from the fire. Even in its dim glow, my red cheeks may give away my embarrassment. "This is the only gown I carry with me, and the jewelry seemed appropriate for a banquet."

He starts to laugh, then clutches his head. "Do not amuse me, Ilena. My head can't stand it. Of course it's appropriate. Did you have doubts?"

"I've never been to a banquet before."

He is silent for a time. I can see the questions he

wants to ask. Instead, he says, "Someday I hope you'll tell me about yourself."

My body trembles for a moment, much as it did when he held my arm in the clearing last night. I manage to sound calm. "There is little to tell."

"Those who came asking your status wanted your lineage. I told them they would have to talk with you."

I take a deep breath. It is one thing to play at being a noblewoman with strangers. I want Durant to know the truth. "I do not know my lineage."

He considers this in silence for a few minutes. Then he asks, "Where were you born? There is no fortress that I've heard of in the Vale of Enfert."

"I don't know. I was only a few days old when my parents carried me into the Vale of Enfert."

"Have you visited in the East before?"

"No. This is the first time I've been in a fortress or a great hall or a house with separate rooms." It does not seem so difficult to speak with Durant about this.

His voice is soft. "We will go to Dun Alyn as soon as I can travel."

"I will leave tomorrow," I say. "You must wait for word from Arthur, and his orders may not let you travel to the East."

He sighs. "That is true. My first allegiance is to my chief and whatever task he assigns me."

"I wish to go on at once. Snow is expected, and the high passes fill quickly."

"I will ask Chief Perr to send someone with you."

"That is not necessary."

"Do you know the route through the mountains?"

I admit that I do not.

"The road is said to be easy to follow once you are over the last pass. Perr should be able to send someone that far with you."

"I would welcome help." The trip had seemed simple enough at first. I planned to keep moving east on the main trails and hoped to find a farm or village if I needed to ask directions. It would be a great help to have a guide lead me through the mountains and point out the trail the rest of the way.

There are voices outside, in the central portion of the house. The men who have come in are talking about Dun Alyn. I step close to the doorskin to hear better.

"And Belert can't stay in charge anyway."

"Who is next with Miquain gone?"

"Ogern has a granddaughter."

"Bad luck, that."

Durant asks, "What are they saying?"

I repeat what I've just heard and then tell him what the bard sang about the ladies of Dun Alyn. I can hear the men settling in beside the central fire. It is time for me to return to the women's quarters, but I hesitate for a moment. It is pleasant here with Durant, and I realize I'm not eager to leave alone in the morning.

"I will come back before I ride out tomorrow." I reach for the doorskin.

"Ilena." His voice sounds like Moren's when he

wanted to order me to do something but knew I would rebel. "I wish you would wait here for me. Arthur may send word that I should go to Dun Alyn. Even if he does not, I will go with you if I can."

I hold the edge of the deerskin and rub my thumb over the sleek fur while I think. It is warm here, with good food and a soft bed. A companion on the trail would be wonderful. But I remember Moren repeating over and over, "Plan carefully. Then don't let anything lead you astray."

I force myself to speak firmly. "That is two *ifs*, Durant. One that you would be free to go and the other that snow will hold off to allow travel."

"You would be safer."

"And I might be trapped here as a guest all winter."

"Well, there are those who would welcome your company."

I laugh. "That is ridiculous. I'm not looking for a husband."

I drop the doorskin behind me and hurry across the center of the house. The conversation by the fire stops as I walk past and resumes as I go through the outer door.

I sleep well, and when I awaken, I can see morning light around the shutters. I'd like to slip out quickly to Rol and be on my way, but leaving without goodbyes to my hosts would be rude. And I want to see Durant again.

I open the shutters and look out to brisk sunshine. The building across a patch of courtyard must be a stable. I hear a horse and the jingle of harness. A man in a checked cloak rides a tall black horse across the far end of the courtyard. I lean out the window, but he is gone from my sight almost at once.

The doorskin moves behind me, and I hear Gola's cheerful voice. "Good morning, lady. Chief Perr and his wife ask that you join them, and Durant sends word that he waits for you."

"Am I the last one abed in the fortress?" It must have been the ale or two days of travel. I remember nothing after slipping in as quietly as possible last night and removing my dress and jewelry.

"Not quite. Some still sleep, but most have risen early and gone on a hunt." This morning she is dressed in leather trousers and a short tunic. Her hair is braided into a tight plait down her back.

I yawn and stretch. "I hoped for an early start myself, but I have missed it."

"Perr has asked us to ride with you through the high passes," she says. "My husband knows the trails well and will set you on the track to Dun Alyn before we turn back."

"That is good news indeed."

"We'll spend two nights on the trail, and you'll arrive at Dun Alyn in early afternoon the day after tomorrow." She picks up my blue gown and shakes it smooth, then folds it into a tidy bundle for my pack. "Can I do anything to help you?"

"One thing. Someone rode out this morning on a

tall black horse. I thought I saw him last night. He wears a cloak with large brown-and-black checks."

She nods. "I know the one you mean, a stranger to us. He arrived soon after you came yesterday and asked hospitality. He was in the hall for dinner but left early."

"I thought I saw him there."

"You have seen him before?"

"Yes. He passed by the Vale of Enfert several days before I left."

"A traveler from one place to another," Gola says.

I remember the way he stared at me that morning, but I say only, "Perhaps. It is of no matter."

Gola takes my pack and my sword and shield to the stable for me while I head for the Great Hall.

My farewells and thanks to Chief Perr and his wife take time.

"You'll give our regards and our sympathy to Belert?" Faren asks.

"Of course," I answer, though I doubt that I will be talking with the chief of Dun Alyn for any reason.

I assure them that I will return to Dreug again as soon as I can. At last I leave them and hurry to Durant's quarters.

Sun is streaming through the window onto his bed, and he sits with his back against the wall. The bandage over his eye is smaller today.

"You look well," I say. "The swelling is down."

"Perhaps I will return to normal. I would like to go with you today."

"Gola and her husband will take me through the high passes."

"That will put you a few hours from Dun Alyn. I am worried about what you will find."

"Why?"

"The bard you heard at dinner came to talk with me last night after you left. He is a friend to Arthur's cause. He spoke of turmoil in Belert's hall. There is a fight brewing over Belert's claim as chief."

"How could that be?" I have heard many stories of disputes over a chief's right to rule but rarely understood the issues clearly.

"Belert has two claims to the leadership of Dun Alyn. One is simply the agreement of those he leads. Any strong protest by the warriors could displace him. Belert pleases his followers; he is brave and wise. The war band follows him gladly."

"What is the problem, then?"

"The second claim is by succession. As long as the woman who inherits the land and all its buildings and cattle grants him the position, he is chief. Belert's wife, Cara, was the true owner of Dun Alyn. Her daughter, Miquain, would have succeeded her. As her father, Belert would still be chief until Miquain chose a husband."

"Of course," I say. "Succession is always from the mother to the daughter."

Durant smiles. "Well, not always. Britons in the

South follow the Roman ways. Men own the land and leave it to their sons."

I am surprised. "That is a strange custom."

"That is what those in the South say of the northern ways."

"Who, then, owns Dun Alyn with Cara and Miquain dead?"

"That is the problem. Dun Alyn's Druid, Ogern, is uncle to Cara. He has a granddaughter. The bard says Ogern will push her claim."

"And what would happen to Belert?"

"He might go back to his own people. But there is no guarantee that Ogern would allow him to leave Dun Alyn alive."

"You mean, he would keep him prisoner?"

"Or send him to the Oak Grove for the sacrifices. Belert is a Christian and supports all who practice the faith. If Ogern can get rid of him, many would return to the old ways."

I remember the stories I heard as a child and feel a shiver through my body.

"Will you wait till I can go with you?" Durant asks. "Perr would welcome you here all winter if the snows come."

I speak as firmly as I can. "No. I must go." Two emotions battle inside me. I am eager to be on my way, but leaving Durant is difficult.

"Then God be with you."

"And with you," I respond. I turn to the door but stop when he speaks again.

"I owe you much, Ilena. If you had not come along when you did . . ."

"Bork was doing well."

"He could not have held them off forever. Wherever I live the days of my life, I will know that you have given them to me." He stops, looking, it seems, for words. "We are bound, you and I. Between God and myself, I am from this day your brother. Whatever my sister needs, I will give; whenever you call, I will come. Wherever you go, know that Durant, Chief of Hadel and liege to Arthur, is your foster brother and protector."

I gulp. This is no small oath. "I have longed for a kinsman. It is an honor to be your sister." I reach out to take his hand in the clasp of friendship. His arm is warm where I grasp it, and the curly red hairs prickle my arm where it lies against his. I try again to speak, but I cannot get words out.

He says, "I will follow you to Dun Alyn when I can."

I nod and leave quickly so he won't see my distress.

CHAPTER 6

It is a cool day, and the sun flits out of clouds overhead to gleam from time to time on the lake. Our path lies along the cliff for a short distance, then slopes down to touch the shoreline at the easternmost end of the long water.

Gola and her husband, Cochan, lead the way. Cochan is a huge man with a bright yellow mustache and yellow hair plastered back off his face with lime in the old manner. Despite the chill wind and hint of rain in the air, he wears no tunic or shirt under his leather war vest, and his burly arms glisten with perspiration. Tattoos ripple across his chest and shoulders. A leather war helmet hangs from his saddle beside a large bronze shield.

The brush of orange fur knotted around his left arm marks him as one who honors the fox. It would be a taboo for him to hunt a fox, as he has sworn kinship with those brave and wily creatures. Harming one, even accidentally, would bring great ill fortune to him.

Gola wears her helmet, as do I. We have both bound our plaited hair up out of sight in the usual manner of women away from shelter, though it is hard to imagine a danger that Cochan couldn't handle. While we ride, his head turns constantly as he watches the trail, the trees around us, and the hills above. We move single file down the steep incline to the lake shore with Cochan in the lead and Gola behind him. On level ground he falls back to ride alongside her. A trace of a smile lightens his stern face when he catches her eye, and once I see him reach out to touch her arm in a soft caress.

Soon we are moving briskly by a wide stream that flows into the lake from a source high in the hills above. There is room now for us to ride three abreast, and my escorts fall back to flank me. They ride brown mares so alike I can't tell one from the other.

"Sisters," Gola says. "Mine is the older one. They were wedding gifts from Cochan's family."

"Do any mistake them for twins?" I ask. People in the Vale of Enfert observe the taboo that forbids twins to live. When one of our cows birthed twins, Moren kept cow and calves in the barn for a time. Villagers heard about it and began coming, first in twos and threes, then all together in a large group. Moren ordered me into the house with Grenna and stalked down the path to meet them. I listened hard but could hear only snatches of conversation.

"... curse upon us all."

"The Druids say ..."

"... must be killed ..."

At last Moren returned with a grim look on his face. He said nothing, and Grenna didn't ask, but the next morning he saddled his big stallion. Grenna and I lifted the larger calf up to him; Moren held it over the horse's withers while Grenna tied the little legs together. The animal's piteous bawls faded as they rode over the pass and out of sight. Moren returned late that night with a crate of chickens tied behind his saddle and two bags of oats slung where the calf had been.

I was afraid to ask what had happened, but he knew my feelings. "Don't worry, lass. I found a farmer whose cow lost her calf just yesterday. Our wee one has a good home." Grenna had worried as much as I; her eyes filled with tears, and she turned away quickly.

Now Cochan laughs at my question. "No one questions me about my horses," he says.

The stream beside us has narrowed and splashes loudly. When our trail curves sharply away to the left, Cochan stops us and points to a faint track that continues alongside the rushing water.

"Your well is there. I'll wait here."

Gola says, "I want to visit Mona's Well. It is not far. Will you go with me?"

"Of course," I answer. Grenna and I went often to

the Sacred Well near the end of the Vale of Enfert. Fiona went with me the day before I left so we could ask protection for my journey.

We ride single file alongside the stream for a few minutes and come to a dark grove. Oaks surround the space, and their branches intertwine to block out the sunlight. A slight breeze rustles the brown leaves above us. The well is deep in shadow, but I can make out a skull set just above the water.

We dismount and tie the horses to a sapling. I look around and think of the ceremonies that must have taken place under these trees. "Do the Druids sacrifice here?" I ask.

"Not any longer," Gola answers. "The rituals are held in another grove; Dun Dreug hasn't practiced human sacrifice for years. We come here only to pray at the well and to watch the Druid cut the sacred plants." She points up into an ancient oak, and I can see bright green leaves of mistletoe gleaming against the dark tree bark.

When I lower my eyes, I'm staring straight at the skull in its niche across the spring. I shudder and look away.

Gola's war vest and helmet are on the ground beside her, and she holds her tunic up. Her trousers are loosened so that her abdomen is exposed.

"Will you help me?" she asks.

Fiona and I often assisted our older friends with the ritual for fertility. I know how to sprinkle water over a woman's body to bring the blessing of the water spirits. I reach down into the pool for a handful of water.

"No, no," she says. "With the head."

I look at the skull.

"It won't hurt you. Mona brings luck to all who wish to bear a child."

I reach across the spring and take the skull. It feels cool and clammy. I dip up water and splash it out of the skull's mouth onto Gola's belly. She flinches from the cold shock but says nothing. I set the skull down and take her hand.

We walk slowly around the spring sunwise with the water always at our right hands. When we get back to the skull again, I splash more water over her. Nine times we silently repeat the rite.

After I replace the skull, we bow to the spring, and Gola reties her trousers and puts on her helmet and vest.

She glances at the sun overhead. "Let's hurry. Cochan will be impatient."

He is sitting against a tree, waiting for us. "About time," he says. His tone is gruff, but his face softens when he looks at Gola. There are splotches of water on her tunic and trousers, and she is shivering. Before he mounts his horse, he pulls her cloak from the top of her pack and hands it to her. "Wear this till you dry off."

The trail slopes gradually upward until we reach a steep ascent. Cochan stops us near a stream that rushes down the mountain. "We'll rest here. It's hard going up that track." He nods toward a jumble of rocks that rises as high as I can see. The path is clear enough here at the bottom but disappears quickly in the mass of boulders.

"It looks impossible," I say.

Gola laughs. "Just difficult. There's another tomorrow that is worse."

"I'm glad you came with me."

"Chief Perr knew we'd like a few days to ourselves." Gola smiles at Cochan.

I reckon they have not been married long. It is a warming feeling to see a couple so fond of each other.

I think again of Grenna and Moren and the looks, the smiles, the gentle touching when they thought I wasn't watching. I feel an ache inside. The Vale of Enfert is the only home I've known, though I was an outsider there. With Moren and Grenna gone, I was alone there, too. Even with Jon I would have felt out of place. How good it must feel to have someone, to belong somewhere.

We share our midday meal sitting against a sun-warmed rock and watching a pair of peregrine falcons overhead. They swoop in great slow circles over the moor and then hang motionless far above us. The horses drink from the stream and crop grass along its bank. There is a cold wind coming down the mountainside. I pull my cloak tight around me and shut my eyes.

"Ilena, wake up." Gola shakes my shoulder gently.

I jump up, embarrassed to find I'd fallen asleep.

Cochan hands me Rol's rein. "We'll walk up this. It's steep for the horses even without riders."

Steep it is. The path is a narrow opening between huge boulders and piles of scree. In many places I have to scramble on hands and knees to get over rough spots. Cochan is far ahead, and Gola follows me. I've dropped Rol's rein. There is no place for him to go except straight up with me, and he follows gamely. The mares are agile and seem accustomed to this kind of climbing. At least they don't roll their eyes and snort as often as Rol does.

We pause at the summit for a few minutes to rest before starting down the east side of the mountain.

Our night shelter is a small, enclosed space; the walls are a welcome break against the cold wind. Gola builds a tiny fire against the inner wall while Cochan and I rub down the horses and measure out three piles of oats. Water runs down a crevice in the stone to a small pool. Rol and the mares drink deeply before they start on the oats.

There is little space for our sleeping places. I spread Rol's saddle blanket as far from Gola and Cochan as I can, and I look without success for any vegetation to soften the hard rock beneath it.

"It's a hard sleep here," Gola says.

"Aye, and a short one," adds Cochan. "We need to be up at first light to make the next pass tomorrow."

We eat in silence. Stars are thick in the clear, dark sky; water from the little cascade tastes of mountain ice. I fall asleep the instant I lie down.

When I awaken in the dim predawn light, Cochan is harnessing the horses, and I hear a murmured comment from Gola in their sleeping place.

"I'm awake," I call softly.

"High time," he says. "You women are a problem. Sleep all day if I'd let you."

I feel a flash of anger at his tone but relax at the sound of Gola's laugh.

By noon we have made some headway up the stony slopes of the next mountain range. Cochan assures me that we will find shelter just over the pass by sundown. I struggle on, thinking of Moren. It is no wonder he returned exhausted from his journey. I wish he were beside me now.

Night camp is another rocky hollow with wind howling around us. I measure Rol's grain carefully. There is no grass to crop up here, and the tiny pile of oats I pour for him is soon gone. There is enough left in the sack for tomorrow morning. I notice Gola weighing their grain sack after she feeds the mares.

She says, "I think we could spare a little if Rol needs more."

I'm touched by her offer. Grain for the animals is a difficult matter; it is heavy to carry, but necessary if they are to remain strong. "Thank you. He has enough, and you have two days' travel to return to Dun Dreug."

"You'll find a good meadow at the bottom of this trail," Cochan says. "He'll have grazing by noon tomorrow."

It is a shock to remember that they will leave me tomorrow. My face must show my concern. Gola reaches out to touch my arm.

"Do you want us to go on to Dun Alyn with you, Ilena?"

I swallow hard. Of course I want them to stay with me. As I come closer to Dun Alyn, I begin to fear what I will find. I force myself to sound calm.

"I will miss you, but I will be fine. You are needed back at Dun Dreug." I manage a smile.

She looks worried. My smile must not be very reassuring.

Cochan speaks. "Your kin will be glad to see you. How long has it been since you've seen them?"

"Oh, years," I say with as light a tone as I can manage. Do I even have kin there? The closer I get to the end of the trip, the more unlikely that seems. Where will I find the woman called Ryamen? How do I approach the gates of Dun Alyn?

"We'll go on in the morning till you can see the trail," Cochan says. "There is an outcrop that gives a view clear to the sea. I'll point the direction when we get there."

I sleep soundly again and waken to Cochan's bustle about the horses. I watch closely this morning and notice that, despite his gruffness, he is moving quietly to let us sleep longer. Gola is a lucky woman.

The outcrop is only an hour's trek down the eastern slope of the mountain. The sun lightened the early-morning sky but now has retreated behind a sullen cloud cover. Rain falls on plains to the south. Far to the east I can see the ocean. It looks flat and gray from so far away, but I'm sure the waves churn as fiercely as they do on the western coast near the Vale of Enfert.

Cochan points down the slope below us. A trail meanders around piles of boulders and sharp drop-offs. It disappears from view in places, then can be seen again farther down. The constant switchbacks look to be an easier descent than the one we stumbled through yesterday. At the foot of the mountain a wide valley stretches, green and inviting.

Cochan draws my attention to the northeast. "See that pine forest just past the mouth of the valley?"

I nod. The conifers make a dense green pattern in the surrounding browns and yellows.

"Dun Alyn lies on the coast. Follow the stream in the valley below us till it meets a river. The crossing is downstream a short distance. From there the track leads into that forest. Stay on the main trail and you will come to a clearing where the trail branches in two directions. The right one leads to Dun Alyn."

Gola says. "I could go on with Ilena."

"And then you'd return alone," Cochan says. "Ilena's route is easy. She'll have no trouble finding her way."

"You can use that sword you carry?" Gola asks.

I manage a laugh that I hope sounds convincing and say, "Yes, of course."

Cochan touches Gola on the arm and motions back up the trail. She follows him slowly. I take Rol's lead rein over my shoulder and turn down the path.

When I look back from the first bend, she's watching me. We wave and turn to our separate paths. I go on alone.

CHAPTER 7

JUST A FEW DAYS AGO I HADN'T MET GOLA OR DURANT. Yet I miss them as sorely as I miss Jon and Fiona.

To add to my gloom, the skies, which have threatened all morning, open and pour down a cold deluge. I clutch my cloak tight around me, and Rol shakes his head against the pounding rain. The path down the mountainside has become a stream. It is hard to know where to step through the rushing water.

I see a dark place in the cliffs and I turn Rol from the path in hope of shelter. It is a cave that opens into the rock face. The space inside is high enough for us to stand. A fire circle is in the center and a low ledge holds pine boughs. This must be a popular spot for night camp.

The rain continues outside the opening, but it is dry inside. Even with Rol's steamy body heat in the shelter, I begin to shiver. I must start a fire to dry my clothes and warm my body before we can go on. I rummage on the ledge for the oldest bits of pine boughs. When I put them on the fire circle, I discover a few live coals under the ashes. Someone has been here recently.

I blow the coals into life and add more boughs from the bedding. Rol backs into a corner of the cave as far as possible from the blaze. I hang my wet cloak over the ledge closest to the fire and take my pack off of his back; the skins around it have protected the contents. After changing into a dry tunic, I drape my damp trousers and vest on the ledge and put my wet boots as near the blaze as I dare. Rol has shaken and stomped until he is dry. At last I begin to feel warm.

Sheets of water are falling outside the cave entrance. Cochan said I would be at the gates of Dun Alyn soon after noon. That assumed I would travel steadily. I've lost time sitting here, and the mud and puddles underfoot will slow me even more.

I consider my arrival at Dun Alyn. At Dun Dreug I was taken for an important person because I rode in with Durant. I'll be alone and unknown at Dun Alyn. Looking good enough to impress those I meet will be difficult in my mud-stained boots and trousers. I look over the things in my pack. The bracelets would slide about and tangle in the reins; the circlet for my hair won't fit under my helmet. I study the torc.

The shapes carved into the end pieces look like faces. They stare back at me, and seem to hold knowledge I cannot fathom. The piece was appropriate at

Dun Dreug. It won't interfere with handling a horse or weapons. The torcs were designed for heroes to wear in battle. Moren told stories of warriors saved from an enemy's sword blow because the blade caught the torc instead of flesh.

I think of Moren and his last words to me. Will I find Ryamen? And how do I gain entrance to the fortress? There will be gates and sentries.

A ray of sun catches the doorway. The rain has stopped. I clasp the torc around my neck and put everything else back in the pack. I pull on my damp boots, trousers, and vest and lead Rol out of the cave.

The path is treacherous. Rol slips several times. I lose my footing often. Once I fall flat in a wide puddle and add a generous layer of mud to my already soiled clothing. At least the sun is warm, so I do not need my damp cloak to keep away the cold.

When we reach the valley, I stop beside the stream and scrape off some of the mud. After Rol drinks, he begins cropping grass. I remove his bit so he can graze in comfort. When he has eaten steadily for a time, I mount and ride on. It feels good to be on horseback again after so much clambering up and down rocky trails. Rol, too, enjoys the level path, and we make good time to the river crossing. The water is shallow and he splashes across with no hesitation.

The trail leads into deep shadows under dense pines. The trees are old, with high branches, and I can stay mounted with a little ducking and dodging.

According to Cochan, the path to Dun Alyn lies through a clearing on the edge of these woods. When I see open space ahead, I hurry Rol on instead of stopping to listen and look around as I should. That is why I miss the first sounds of other people.

We are almost out of the trees when I hear the clink of metal against metal. I pull Rol up, but it is too late. A mounted war band in the clearing has seen me. They are spread out across both paths that branch from the one I'm on.

I wheel Rol to return to the woods, but a man on a large black horse blocks the path behind me. He stares at me from under the brass-trimmed helmet with the same intensity he showed in the Vale of Enfert. I would recognize him even without the checked cloak bundled behind his saddle. I can see his face clearly now; he has heavy brows over hard brown eyes and a full black mustache. He sits his horse firmly, and there is no way around him.

"No." His voice is deep and smooth. "You'll not escape this way, lady."

I whirl Rol around toward the clearing and see the war band moving toward me with spears ready. I haven't time to get one of my war spears. I sweep my shield into my left hand along with the reins and take my sword in my right hand. Rol leaps forward at my command, and I head him straight for the center of the line in front of me.

Five warriors are advancing across the clearing. All

wear the blue facial tattoos of the painted ones from the Far North. The man in the center and another beside him ride tall horses. The others—two men, one woman—ride ponies.

I urge Rol on and begin the war cry Moren taught me. The sound takes the five in front of me by surprise. I call more loudly and keep Rol headed straight for the center of the line. The man there has his war spear held firmly to the front. As we come close, I signal Rol with my knees; he swerves just out of range of the spear and rears to bring his hooves down on the other horse's hindquarters. The animal bolts and throws its rider.

I call out the war cry again and hear it echo through the forest. Our momentum has carried us through the group. I urge Rol onto the right-hand path and find that the man on the black horse has moved to block my way.

This time he has sword in hand and starts toward me. "You should have stayed in your western valley," he says.

As I prepare to meet him, a spear point thrusts against my vest from the back. I topple sideways but manage to stay in the saddle. Rol feels my body shifting and responds by backing away from both attackers. The spear fails to pierce the heavy leather, and I strike with my shield edge against the painted warrior's spear arm. He backs away to set his spear again.

The battle cries that come from the woods around

us cannot be echoes. The old words, so familiar to me, ring out shrill and threatening from at least a dozen voices. The man on the black horse is within sword's reach. As the calls intensify, he pulls his mount up short and jerks it around to gallop down the path toward Dun Alyn.

I give my attention to the painted one charging on my left. I catch the spear point on my shield and push my attacker off balance. My sword strikes his shoulder, and he falls with a scream.

When I turn toward the others, a slingstone smashes against my forehead just below my helmet. I reel from the blow and can see nothing but bright bursts of light for several moments. I try to swing my sword before me to fend off attackers, but I cannot lift it high enough to clear Rol's head.

I am unable to defend myself and brace for a death blow. I hear metal strike metal, and the battle cries are deafening. Finally my eyes clear, and I see that a large war band has entered the clearing from the left fork. Those who attacked me are fighting now for their own lives.

Some of the newcomers break past the skirmishes and surround me until I'm protected by a ring of warriors. The pain in my head worsens, and the blinding light bursts begin again. I slump forward over Rol's neck and feel my sword fall from my hand.

CHAPTER 8

WHEN I OPEN MY EYES AGAIN, I AM LYING ON THE ground. My helmet is off, and a cold cloth presses on my forehead. The noise of battle is gone, and I hear several voices close by.

"Back to help Belert, I'd guess."

"A problem for Ogern, this."

"He's the Druid. He'll know what it means."

"I'm not getting close. Not to that."

The words make no sense to me. My head throbs, and I move to ease it. A moan escapes. Someone presses a waterskin against my lips.

"She drinks like one of us."

"Aye," the man holding the waterskin says, "and bleeds like us too."

"And what about that torc?"

"I've not seen it for years." He takes the waterskin down. "Enough now?"

I try to nod, but the pain stops me. "Thank you."

I open my eyes and focus on the man beside me.

He is near Moren's age, with sweat-soaked hair matted against his head from the leather helmet that lies beside him. He watches me closely. He offers bread from a pack beside him. "Do you eat?"

A strange question. In answer I reach out for the bread and break it in two. I hand him back one of the pieces and take a bite from the other. It is stale and tastes of leather from his pack, but I hope eating will cure the strange weakness I feel. I force myself to sit up. My head swims, but the pain is lessening. I think for a moment of Durant and wonder if he is recovering. At least I can see out of both eyes.

Two other men sit against trees nearby. One wraps a point onto a war spear. The other, a youth little older than I, stares at me with wide eyes. I can hear more voices and the sound of horses a short distance away.

The man beside me removes the compress. "Does it hurt, lady?"

"Some." Words jar against the pain.

"Cormec, you're a braver man than I." The young man stands. "You and Toole stay here if you like. I'll be out with the others."

"Tell them we'll move on shortly." He turns to me. "Will you be able to ride?"

"Yes. I think so." Am I their prisoner? Who are these men? The two shields I see are large and round, with scrolls worked around a band of animals. They are much like mine. I swallow the last of the little piece of bread and reach out for the waterskin.

He hands it to me and asks, "And should we send word on to the chief?"

I consider this. I must not be a prisoner if my advice is sought. "As you wish," I say. Cormec and Toole exchange glances. I should have said something else.

Cormec speaks. "Get our horses, Toole. We'll try to make Dun Alyn by dark."

These, then, are Dun Alyn's people. That explains the battle cry. The call I learned from Moren is the war cry of Dun Alyn.

It seems strange that no one has asked my name or lineage.

Toole eyes the spear he's refitted and tucks a sinew end into the binding. Only then does he unfold himself to stand above us. "And shall I have the horns blow?"

"Aye, of course," Cormec says. "My mind is elsewhere."

Toole nods and disappears into the trees. In a few minutes I hear war horns sound a quick rhythm, and there is a general bustle. Toole returns leading three horses.

I take a deep breath and lift myself to my feet.

Rol has been rubbed down. A scratch on his croup is freshly salved, and my sword rests in its scabbard on the saddle.

I turn to pick up my helmet and shield, but Cormec is ahead of me. "Let me, lady." He hands them to me.

I hang them both on harness fittings and clamber into the saddle. The rest of the troop waits at the fork. Talking stops when we appear, and all eyes are on me. Two young men nod to Cormec and swing onto the trail toward Dun Alyn. The three of us follow them. The rest of the band falls in behind us.

It is dark when we approach Dun Alyn. The moon has yet to rise, and I cannot see to guide Rol. He matches pace with the mounts on either side of me.

Light from torches and evening fires glows above the walls. A stiff sea breeze brings smoke and the scent of food along with its salt tang. We move out of tree cover and climb a steady ascent to the first gateway. The watch has seen us, and torches flare.

"Well met, Cormec," someone calls. "We've been expecting you for hours."

"Who is that with you?" Another voice speaks.

A torch pushes close. I can see the man who holds it. He stares at me, then speaks in a hushed voice. "By the gods, Cormec. How can it . . . ?"

The sentries step back to let us pass. Their eyes never leave me.

The entrance to the inner wall is wide enough for six horsemen or two chariots side by side. I think of the story of Cara and Miquain; this is where they rode to their deaths. Huge stockade gates secure the opening. When we halt with the first horses' noses almost touching the pales, a voice sounds from the other side.

"Yo! And shall we open?"

The others look to Cormec. He answers with words I do not recognize. It must be a password. The gates open. These sentries stare as intently as those at the outer entrance.

"Is the chief at meat?" Cormec asks.

"Of course. Though it's said he eats almost nothing now."

"We must see him at once."

One of the sentries hurries away ahead of us.

The compound grounds stretch a long way into the darkness. There are fires here and there on the ground. Small homes cluster near the walls, and light from their inside fires glows out of windows and doors. Larger buildings take shape in the distance, and we head for the largest.

I had hoped for time to compose myself, to wash, and to replait my hair. I need to think of what I will say to explain myself.

There is to be no opportunity. We ride directly across the grounds and dismount at the entrance to the Great Hall. I find that my knees are weak, and I cannot walk without stumbling. No one reaches out to assist me.

The doorkeeper blocks our entrance for a short time while he considers me. Finally he shakes his head in what looks to be bewilderment and motions us through the door. I gulp deep breaths in an effort to steady myself.

This hall is larger than the one at Dun Dreug. Dining has finished; a bard is playing as we step inside. The warm scent of cooked meats still hangs in the smoky air. Fires blaze in hearths throughout the room, though shutters are open to the night breezes.

Those nearest the door see us first. There is silence, then a wave of comments.

"By the gods!"

"It can't be!"

"Where . . . ?"

And from someone off to the right: "The torc! The Great Torc of Dun Alyn."

I call on strength I didn't know I had and begin the long walk to the dais at the far end of the room. My head spins from the wound, and my knees tremble from fear at this strange reception. I force my head high; whatever may happen, no one can say I look the coward. Cormec stays beside me but offers no hand of support. When my arm accidentally touches Toole's, he flinches and drops behind us.

By the time Cormec and I reach the platform, I cannot hear any more talking. The music has stopped, and the room is silent save for the snap of branches in the hearth fire and a rustle as people turn to follow our progress.

The man at the center of the table raises himself

slowly from an elaborately carved chair. He must be Chief Belert. I am conscious of the bloody wound on my forehead, the strands of hair that fall loose around my face, and the mud caked on my trousers. I square my shoulders and return his gaze with as much dignity as I can muster.

"Who . . . who are you?" The words seem to come with difficulty. He holds on to his chair back for support, and I can see that his knuckles are white against the dark wood. The beard and curly hair that frame his face are gray with traces of brown. His eyes look blue, though it is difficult to see clearly in the torchlight.

He looks to the man beside me. "Explain this, Cormec!"

I am relieved to have the attention shift. I have dreaded questions, have pondered how to answer them. I still have no idea. My head hurts, and dizziness makes thinking difficult.

Cormec is speaking. "We were coming from the north toward the fork. We heard the battle cry. We looked at each other, and no one could say who might be calling. The voice sounded like one we knew. The words were clear."

"You could not have been mistaken?"

"No, Belert. It was our call."

"When you heard the call what did you do?"

"We raised the cry ourselves and urged our mounts toward the battle. What else would we do?"

The chief sighs. "Cormec, I do not criticize. I am trying to understand this."

There are only two other people at the table. One is a girl some years younger than I. Her wiry black hair, much like mine, and something about her face remind me of Moren. She twists a strand of hair with one finger and stares at me with wide eyes.

The tall man beside her has piercing gray eyes and the high shaved forehead of a Druid. His long gray hair falls forward in tangles around his face. He rises and points a long finger at me. "There is nothing to understand, Belert. This shapeshifter has come among us for no good. We must send her back to her unnatural companions."

"Hold on, Ogern." The chief's voice is sharp. "I will hear the rest of Cormec's story. And then I will hear from the lass herself."

Ogern raises his voice to a shout. "It is not a lass. It is an evil one from the other world. We dare not give her opportunity to weave her spells."

"Sit down, Ogern. I will hear Cormec out."

There are murmurs behind me. Ogern has stirred the fears of some in the hall. He sits but keeps his eyes on me.

The room quiets as Cormec's steady voice continues. "We reached the clearing at the fork. Five from beyond Red Mountain had attacked this one. I saw her charging and wielding her sword like a true warrior.

Just as we reached the battle, she was hit in the head with a slingstone."

"Did you recognize her?"

Cormec hesitates. "I don't know about the others. I saw the horse—certainly one from our lines—and the torc. I have not seen that torc for years, but I knew it at once. The lady wore a low helmet, and her hair was hidden. In truth she could have been a lad. Yet there was much about her that spoke to me even so."

"And you engaged her attackers?"

"Of course. There was no question in any of our minds. It happened fast, but our allegiance was clear. We formed the fighting ring around her and dispatched the others."

"There were five of them?"

Cormec is silent for a moment. Then he speaks slowly. "Toole was ahead of me into the clearing. He thought he saw someone vanish down the path toward Dun Alyn."

Belert looks back into the gloom at the back of the hall. "Toole?"

Toole comes forward to stand beside Cormec. He casts a worried glance at me. "Yes, my chief."

"You saw someone?"

"Yes. I could not make out the man—or woman—but I saw a black horse disappear into the trees. The lady could tell us."

"We cannot listen to her. She speaks evil from the

land of spirits." Ogern has risen again. His voice thunders across the hall.

"Ogern, you forget yourself. I am chief here." Belert's voice is firm.

Ogern sits down. His eyes, through the wild gray tangles that frame his face, burn with a frightening intensity when he looks at me.

Belert speaks then to Cormec and Toole. "What happened after the battle?"

Cormec looks to Toole, who shakes his head. Cormec sighs and says, "The lady was hurt. She'd dropped her sword."

"What sword?" Belert's voice is sharp. "Was it . . . ?" he stops.

Cormec seems to know what he means. "No. Her sword is like that one. A fine blade from Trelawn's forge, but I had not seen it before."

"But she was hurt? As a mortal is hurt?" He glares at Ogern as he speaks.

"Yes. We—I—removed her helmet. No one else would come near."

"And wise they were," Ogern says.

"And you, Cormec, are a courageous man," Belert says.

"I could not leave her to suffer. The helmet was pressing on the swelling."

"Did she drink? Or eat?"

"Aye. Both."

"And I tell you spirits can eat and drink and feign wounds and whatever else suits their evil purpose," Ogern says.

Belert ignores him and looks at me. I feel weak and sad, somehow, when I encounter his eyes. "And now, lass, tell us who you are and why you have come to Dun Alyn."

I have no story ready, no way to explain who I am, and no understanding of what is going on around me. I can speak only the truth. I take a deep breath and try to ignore the pounding in my head. "Sir, I am Ilena, of the Vale of Enfert in the West."

He waits for me to say more, then speaks when I do not. "And what is your lineage, Ilena? Who is your mother, and who is your father?"

"Grenna is my mother, and Moren is my father," I say. I see shock on Belert's face. The rest of the hall seems even quieter than it has been. Their names have meaning here.

Ogern shouts, "That tells us well enough where she comes from. Moren and Grenna have been dead for years."

Belert starts to speak but stops and reaches over the carved chair back for his flagon. He drinks deeply, then wipes his mouth. He stares at me in silence for another minute before he asks, "Where are Moren and Grenna now?"

Tears flood my eyes. It is too much. The wound, the animosity I find here, and now the pain of remembering. I force my voice to stay steady. "Grenna died two summers past. Moren died a few days ago. They lie side by side above the Vale of Enfert."

Ogern springs to his feet before Belert can speak. "Lies! Spells from the other world. Moren and Grenna died years ago. Do you remember, Belert?"

"Remember!" The chief's voice is loud enough now for all to hear, but he speaks only to Ogern. "Remember? How could I forget? I returned from a hunting trip to find the baby born before its time and Moren, my war leader and most trusted friend, gone without explanation. I remember, Ogern. I remember."

He turns to the hall. "Moren and Grenna vanished without a trace. Cara told me that Grenna went mad with grief over the loss of her own baby, and the sight of our beautiful Miquain sent her shrieking from the room. Moren took her away to recover. When we heard nothing through the summer, we looked for them."

Ogern steps forward to stand beside the chief. His voice is sharp, and he throws the words out as if they were slingstones. "We sent searchers everywhere. A messenger went south to Grenna's people. No one there had heard from them. Moren and Grenna are long dead, and this shapeshifter comes to do us harm."

"And if Moren and Grenna lived? She could be their child."

"No," Ogern shouts. "Grenna could have no more children. That was why her grief was so deep. The midwife was certain; she would never carry another babe. This one could not be hers."

The words strike me like a blow. Grenna not my mother!

Chief Belert is watching me. His eyes hold sympathy, I think. All there is in this hall, anyway. There is mumbling behind me. Ogern's words find willing ears.

A woman's voice close behind me hisses, "A shapeshifter!"

A man's voice carries above the others. "Bad luck, that. And Samhain Eve in thirteen days."

The chief hears the voices too. He pulls himself straighter and starts to speak. "Good people of Dun Alyn . . ." His voice falters and trails off. He sways and steadies himself by gripping the chair back.

Ogern shoulders him aside and says, "We must act quickly. This spirit that has come among us must not be allowed to bring us harm. It is well known that evil ones take the form of those who have died. It is near Samhain Eve, and the spirits always try to return at this time. If this one stays among us, she can open the doors to a host of her kind who even now roam the world seeking entry into human realms."

Chief Belert steps around him. His voice is weaker now, less certain. "Ogern speaks . . ."

It is no use. Someone nearby calls in a loud voice, "Death! Death! Death to the evil one!" It is a man's voice, deep and familiar.

The chant is taken up throughout the hall. Belert's

face is grim, but he does not try to speak again. He slumps down into his chair and stares at the tabletop.

I shout above the din, "I am not a shapeshifter!" but my voice is lost in the roar.

Ogern's face is triumphant as he looks at me. He lets the noise roll through the hall for several minutes, then holds up his hand for silence. "She will be no danger to us in the Oak Grove."

The chief attempts to stand, but he loses his grip on the chair arms and falls back. He says something, but Ogern drowns him out.

"Cormec, Toole, take her to the sacred grove!"

Toole has stepped back into the shadows. Now he comes forward slowly. Cormec turns to me but makes no attempt to touch me.

I look to Chief Belert. "Sir," I begin, "I am not—"

Ogern cuts me off. His voice rises to a shriek. "We must not let a spirit speak in this hall."

The deep voice begins again behind me. "To the Oak Grove. The sacred grove will keep her."

Others take up the cry until the entire hall is pulsing with the shout. Belert meets my eyes for a moment, then shakes his head as if to clear it and tries to pull himself up again. When he fails, he leans back in his chair and closes his eyes.

Cormec motions to the back of the hall and waits for me to precede him.

Before I can turn around, Ogern speaks again. "Wait. The Great Torc. Get the torc."

Cormec eyes my neck. Toole stands an arm's length from me. Neither makes any move toward the torc.

Ogern walks around the table and steps down from the dais. His long, bony fingers are rough, and one of his nails scratches my throat as he rips the torc from my neck. He carries it back to the table and lays it in front of the girl.

Cormec turns again toward the back of the hall. I turn also, but before I take a step toward the door, I scan the tables near the front of the hall.

He is at a table near the center aisle, just below Ogern's place on the dais. I recognize him without the helmet, without the checked cloak, without the tall black horse. His dark eyes stare at me, and a slight smile plays under the black mustache.

I meet his eyes with defiance, then lift my chin, square my shoulders, and march behind Cormec. Once I am outside the door, my false courage crumbles. I left Rol here only a short time ago, but it seems a lifetime. There are no horses in sight in the courtyard now.

I turn to Cormec. "My horse?"

"In the stables. You won't need him."

I know that those who go to the Oak Groves as prisoners rarely return, but his words shock me all the same. I think of Rol and long to rest my head against his warm neck. Toole has started around the hall toward the back wall. Cormec motions me to follow him.

"Wait, Cormec."

Something in my voice seems to soften him. He looks at me for a moment with sadness.

"Please grant me one request," I say.

"If I can, lady."

"My horse. Care for him and send him, when you can, to Dun Dreug."

"I can do that for you, lady."

"And say that he is for Durant of Hadel. Those at Dun Dreug will know how to reach him. And say that the pack and sword are for Gola. Will you do that for me?" Tears begin now, and I stop trying to talk.

Cormec nods. "Yes, lady. Between myself and God, I will do that for you."

The hall has emptied behind us, and people stream out the wide doors. Most give curious glances in our direction, but no one comes close. Ogern is near the back of the crowd, and he walks beside the man with the dark mustache. They are deep in conversation. The girl follows them.

Ogern seems startled to see us there. He calls to Cormec. "Get her to the Oak Grove before she makes further mischief."

I walk as proudly as I can beside Cormec. It is too dark to see my way, and I stumble on rough ground more than once. Light from torches and fires shows a cluster of houses, and we thread our way among them. As we move past one shuttered window, I hear a child whimpering and a woman's voice singing a soft lullaby. The tears flow harder, and I'm grateful for the darkness that hides my face.

We come out beside the rampart wall, where the smoky torchlight shows a wide ladder leading to the walltop. Cormec and I step around the ladder and head for a gate a few yards ahead of us.

Toole stands talking with three sentries. All turn to stare at me as we approach. Toole takes a torch from one of the sentries and motions to the gate. When it opens, he leads the way out.

CHAPTER 9

THE ROUTE DOWN THE CLIFF AT THE BACK OF THE fortress is steep and rough. The moon still has not risen, and our only light comes from the torch. There are three entrances here, just as there are in the front. All have a night guard posted, and the sentries stare at me with the same half-frightened, half-curious gaze I've encountered from everyone here.

I trip on a rock and fall to my knees just outside the last gate. Toole stands waiting for me to get up by myself. Cormec hesitates for a moment, then reaches out a hand to help me. I nod my thanks.

Stars are bright above us, but I can't take my eyes off the path long enough to determine our direction. At first I hear the sea crash on rocks far below. At the bottom of the slope we enter a dark woods, and I no longer hear the surf. The going is easier, but I am weak and dizzy. The moon has risen when we finally stop on the edge of a small clearing.

A great oak tree stands in the center; its branches cast twisted shadows on the ground. Toole and Cormec step behind me as a tall figure separates itself from the tree trunk and advances toward us.

His face is hidden by the front of a deer skull. Antlers rise from the bony plate on top. The figure sways and seems almost to float. My head swims, and I turn cold.

The stagman speaks. "Who are you?" The voice is Ogern's. "What spirit comes from the Sidth?"

I try to speak, but words won't come.

"Speak!" Ogern comes closer.

I try again. My dry throat feels as it does sometimes in a dream when I want to call out but cannot. Finally I force a few words. "I am not a spirit. I am Ilena. I come from the West Country. Moren is my father. Grenna . . . Grenna is my mother!"

"They have been dead for years. Who are you?"

"I have told you."

"Put her in the pen."

Cormec and Toole move forward and grasp my arms. I struggle to break free but cannot. There is a large wicker cage across the clearing, and they drag me to it. Toole holds me while Cormec takes my dirk out of its sheath and unties my tinderbag. He tugs at the sling and bag of slingstones but leaves them when they don't come loose. Toole's face is grim in the torchlight, but Cormec keeps his face down and does not meet my eyes.

Ogern stands close by while they push me through the door and bar it with heavy poles through the outside latches. Toole moves away with the Druid, but Cormec stands beside my prison for a moment.

"This is all I can do," he mumbles. He raises a pole and pulls the door open far enough to shove something through onto the floor. He replaces the pole, and then he too is gone.

I sweep my hand over the wicker floor and find a waterskin. It holds only a few mouthfuls. I tell myself to save some, but it is gone before my thirst is slaked.

I start by the door and go over every part of the cage. It is woven most tightly around the door, but nowhere is there a space wide enough for my hand. Nothing feels loose; I slam my body into the side walls but cannot even bend them.

Sacrifices take place at night. It is too late for a gathering tonight, so I will have tomorrow to try to think of a plan. I pull my heavy vest off and lie down on it in a corner of the pen.

I try to think about the day. Who is the man with the black mustache, and why does he want me killed? What does Ogern fear about me? And why does he say Grenna could not be my mother? What was the look in Chief Belert's eyes? And do the chanting and shouts in the Great Hall mean everyone thinks I'm a shape-shifter? It all jumbles together and blurs until I can't hold one thought long enough to consider it. Perhaps things will be clearer in daylight.

I've no idea how long I've slept nor, at first, what has awakened me. A sharp feral scent fills my nostrils and chokes me. There is something warm pressing through the wicker against my arm. It feels like Cryner. Something sharp jabs my shoulder, and I force my eyes open. There is enough moonlight to see shadows moving around the cage.

Wolves circle the wicker walls. Their breath steams in the cold air. There are seven of them. The largest has chewed a hole in the woven wall where I was sleeping. It stares at me with steady yellow eyes while its teeth shred the branches. Another has tunneled under the floor. The rest pace around the cage, watching me.

I scramble into the center of the pen. I have no weapon save my sling, and that is useless here. There is no room to swing the leather thong.

The animal digging beneath the floor snuffles loudly and begins chewing on the wicker above its nose. Its body rolls and scrapes in the dirt as it turns its head to reach the plaited branches. The big one gnawing on the corner has enlarged the opening and leans its heavy body against the weakened wall. Two of those circling stop to whine and scratch the cage. All seem to sense that they are closing in.

I choke and cough from the stench. I imagine the smell overwhelming me, those strong white teeth gnawing at me. Durant was right; it was unwise to come alone. He swore to help me, but I have put myself in a place where he can't come to my aid.

I wonder if Fiona and Jon will ever learn what happened to me.

The wolf beneath the floor breaks and gnaws enough of the branches to thrust its nose up through the wicker. It twists and pushes until its whole head is in the cage. I freeze in panic for a moment and then move. As its body pushes through the opening, I scramble behind it and grasp the creature's ear with one hand. I clamp my other arm around its neck and hang on with all my strength. The animal gasps and turns frantically, but I manage to let go of the ear and wrap that arm too around the coarse neck fur.

Moren told me once that wielding the long sword would build muscles equal to any need. I pray that he was right as I thrash around the pen floor trying to keep my grip on the wolf's throat. The stench and flying hairs are choking me, but I hang on as the animal struggles.

The wolves outside the pen howl and lunge against the walls. I can feel the one in my grasp weaken, but the hole at the corner is widening under the weight of two wolves leaping and clawing against it.

The howling rises to a wild shriek. A new note rides above the wolves' voices, a wild keening that sounds like words. The moonlight brightens. A smell of burning pitch mixes with the animal stink.

The corner of the pen breaks, and a wolf falls headlong into the cage. The animal in my arms twists and jerks one last time and is still. When its body goes limp, I drop the lifeless head and push the beast away from me.

The animal in the corner keeps its eyes fixed on my face while it lurches to its feet. I move backward as fast as I can.

"Back up farther." The voice is behind me.

The wolf in the pen with me freezes, then shrinks against the wall.

"The door. It's open. Get out."

The pitch smell and the bright light come from a torch behind me. Afraid to take my eyes off the wolf in the cage, I back slowly toward the voice. An arm circles my waist and swings me through the door. I land sprawled on the ground. A woman steps over me and swings a torch back and forth inside the cage so fast that sparks fly off and shower onto the wolf that cowers there. It stands its ground for a few seconds, then leaps through the opening it made.

There is a glitter of eyes at the side of the clearing. Shapes move in the shadows, and I am alone with the woman.

She stands looking down at me, breathing hard. "Eh, Ilena. Well met—at last." She stretches out her free hand to help me; the torch she holds sputters and smokes above us.

I manage to climb to my feet unaided but grab for

her hand when my knees start to buckle. "I'm . . . I cannot . . ." I stammer in confusion and exhaustion.

She looks at the dead wolf in the enclosure. "You spent your strength well." Gray hair has escaped from the plait at her back and bristles around her face. Soot from the torch streaks the sweat on her forehead. She wears a bronze pendant over her brown dress, and a gray cloak fastened at the shoulder falls behind her. A waterskin and a cloth pouch hang from her belt.

"How do you know me? Who are you?"

"Time enough later for talk. Lean your head here." She tugs until she holds a few hairs.

I flinch from the pain and start to protest.

"Here, where your tunic is torn." She hooks two fingers into the rip at my shoulder and tears out a piece of the cloth.

She hurries around to the hole at the back corner of the cage and hangs the hairs and cloth on sharp pieces of wicker. "Now. Your belt."

I see her plan and pull it off. My scabbard, sling, and bag of stones slide onto the ground. I touch the gold medallion that covers the belt's fastener. Moren gave it to me years ago.

"Hurry. You can get another." She takes it from me and twists the leather into the torn wicker. The medallion glows warmly in reflected torchlight. She reaches inside the pen and fishes out my vest.

I pick up the sling and slide an end through the loop

on the bag of stones, then knot the ends around my waist. I pull on my vest and am grateful for its warmth.

She waves the torch toward a path that leads into the woods. "Come on. Can you hurry?"

I nod and follow her out of the clearing onto a narrow trail through the trees. There is little strength in my body, and each step is an effort. After what seems a great distance, she stops at a stream.

"Drink. You must be thirsty."

I am grateful, both for the water and for a chance to lie flat on the grassy bank for a few minutes. While I drink, she fills her waterskin and returns it to her belt.

Then she whispers, "Stay close to me. Don't talk."

We continue through dark trees on a rough path that comes out onto a meadow. The fortress ramparts loom dark on the hill above us. The woman holds the torch low at her side to hide the light. I wonder why she doesn't douse it in the damp grass, since dawn is upon us.

We pass near a farm enclosure, and a dog barks sharply, startling me. It quiets at a voice from inside the house. We keep up a steady pace down a path that dwindles until I can't tell it from the grassy stretch around it.

When she stops at last, it is at a cromlech that marks a burial mound of the old ones. Three tall stones stand with a flat capstone resting on top of them. Other stones back against the face of an earthen mound. There are no dwellings for as far as I can see.

She leads me in under the capstone and through a narrow doorway between two of the standing stones. Rough-cut steps descend into darkness beneath the mound of earth.

The musty smell of dirt and decay turns my stomach queasy. A narrow stone-floored passage leads down and back into a large room. The flickering torchlight shows skulls on ledges around the walls. Bones are piled in stacks on the rough floor. There is a wide ledge at seat height against one wall.

She holds the torch high to survey the room. "Not very cheerful, this."

I try to answer but have to gulp and get a deep breath before I can force words out. "No. I've never been in a barrow before, but it's better than that cage."

"Aye. Belert and Cara stopped the sacrifices in the Oak Grove years ago. With Cara . . ." She stops and stares at me with a strange, sorrowful expression. She takes a deep breath and begins again. "With Cara gone and Belert's authority weakened, Ogern has begun them again."

"I've heard stories about the groves," I say, "and I didn't want to find out if they were true."

"You hold the new faith, don't you? Moren and Grenna would have seen to that. You know these bones won't hurt you?"

The skulls leer and grimace at me in the dancing shadows. I shudder but say, "I know they have no power. I'll be . . . fine."

"There is a strong taboo against being here for any who hold the old ways. They come only with the Druid for the ceremony each year. No one will look for you in this place."

I nod and try to sound brave. "You called me by name at the grove. How do you know me, and who are you?"

She smiles, and her eyes soften. "I know your name, lass, because I held you when it was given. I am Ryamen."

"Were you with Grenna when I was born, then?" As soon as I see the look on her face, I know that I don't want to hear her answer.

She shakes her head. "Grenna was my dear friend, but . . . What did Moren tell you, Ilena?"

"Nothing. He tried to tell me something, but he was too ill. Just before he died he told me to come east and find you."

She is silent for a few minutes, and there is a far-away look in her eyes. At last she speaks slowly. "Is Moren gone too, then?"

"Yes. Right after he returned. Was he here?"

She nods. "As always, I met him in secret on the second full moon after Lughnasa." She wipes tears from her eyes with the back of her hand.

That explains the urgency about the journeys. At the prearranged time Ryamen would be waiting—looking, I suppose—night after night until he came.

"I was afraid for him this last trip." Her voice is firmer now, but with a new note of sadness. "On the morning he left, one who wishes us harm rode out of the fortress a few hours behind him."

"Who was that?"

She is surprised at my quick question. "Resad, Ogern's friend and ally. They have been busy since Cara's death. Ogern has brought back the worst of the ceremonies in the Oak Grove, and Resad has been away on some mischief."

"Does Resad have a heavy mustache and a tall black horse?"

"Yes. Where have you seen him?"

"He rode into the Vale of Enfert the morning after Moren died. He stared at me strangely, then left. I saw him again when I stopped at Dun Dreug, and he was with those who attacked me yesterday. He led the calls against me in the hall last night."

She nods. "That is why Ogern was so quick to condemn you to the grove, then. The friend who told me of your presence in the hall said that you had no chance to explain and that Belert himself was shouted down. Ogern knew you were coming. Resad must have gathered a war band from outside Dun Alyn to attack you. When that failed he would have hurried to Ogern to let him know you were on your way into the Great Hall."

"But why? Who am I? If Grenna is not my

mother . . ." I am too bewildered to even finish the questions.

Ryamen is apologetic. "I have stayed away too long. The sentry let me out to gather herbs that I said must have the dew on them. They will suspect if I do not return before full light with a bag of plants. Ogern has spies now at all the watches."

"But am I to stay here?" The idea does not please me.

"I will return as soon as the gates open for the day. There is no challenge or question then. We will talk at that time. Your questions are too important to answer quickly."

She reads the expression on my face and hastens to reassure me. "It will only be for a short time." She pulls a small loaf of bread from the pouch and takes the waterskin from her belt. "These will keep you until I return."

I sit down on the ledge and look around me. "Could you please leave the torch?"

She nods and sets it into a niche in the wall. She unfastens the brooch at her shoulder and hands me her cloak. "I'll leave this, too. If the watch notices I don't have it, I'll say I left it where I was gathering herbs." She hesitates a moment, looking at the heavy silver circle in her hand. Then she fastens it onto the cloak. "And you'll need the brooch to clasp it."

"Is there danger for you?" I ask.

She hesitates. "I thought not as long as I drew no particular attention. But if Resad followed Moren to the West and you back here . . ." She stops. "I'll watch carefully when I go back." She reaches out with both hands and grasps my shoulders. "Stay in here. You'll be safe." She embraces me, then turns and hurries down the passage. I can see her silhouette against a patch of light at the entrance as she leaves.

I eat the bread, washing each bite down with a sip of water. The torch sputters and smokes in its niche; soot from old torches streaks the wall around it. The skulls stare down at me. The bones stacked just below the torch look like leg bones.

I take off my vest to pad the ledge, wrap myself in Ryamen's cloak, and lie down. I wish I had my own cloak and Rol's saddlecloth for a pillow. The thought of my horse brings the tears that I've kept back all night. Cormec said he would care for him. Will I see him again? Can Ryamen get me to a safe place?

When I awaken, the torch has died out. I can see the bright patch of sunlight that marks the entrance, but little light penetrates this far back into the mound. I sit up and try moving my head. The pain is gone now, and it feels as if the swelling is down.

It is confusing to be in here with no idea of time; I don't know how long I've slept. I pace back and forth beside the ledge for something to do. I don't dare move away from this small space that is free of bones.

Ryamen was to return as soon as the gates opened at sunup, but the light in the doorway seems too bright for early morning.

Finally I gather my things and move up the passage. When I reach the steps, I hesitate and listen hard for any sound that would mean there are people nearby. At last I step out into the tiny area under the capstone, pressing my body against one of the tall standing stones so I won't be noticed. There is no sign of anyone around. Ryamen said no one would come near a burial mound unless the Druids held ceremonies.

I have a clear view of Dun Alyn in the distance. The tall gates are open, and people come and go on foot, on horseback, and by cart. Figures on a hill beyond the fortress gather hay; smoke trails in the sky mark outlying farms. Insects drone around me.

I squint up at the sun. Since I know that the fortress backs on the eastern sea, I can calculate the directions well enough. The sun has moved long past midday.

Ryamen has not come.

CHAPTER 10

I STAY AGAINST THE TALL STONE, WATCHING UNTIL THE last traces of light disappear in the west. Could Ryamen have come while I slept? She would have awakened me. What can I do now? There is a glow in the sky from the direction of the fortress. Evening fires burn, warming families, cooking the last meal of the day.

A wolf howls from woods nearby. I peer into the darkness of the barrow, but I can't force myself to go back in. It is one thing to know skulls won't hurt me but another to spend the night among them. I spread my vest for a seat beside the door and keep my sling and bag of stones handy in my lap.

The wolf sounds again. This time an answer comes from somewhere on the other side of the earthen mound behind me.

I sit there through the night while the moon rises and wolves howl. A great owl hunts beside the structure, and I hear a rush of wings. A small creature squeals as sharp talons carry it away. Something rustles in grass nearby. I make a slight sound, and the rustling stops.

My tired mind still churns with questions. Why would anyone wish me harm? What did the Druid mean when he accused me of shapeshifting?

I journeyed east to find the place I belong, but I have found a deeper mystery. My presence frightens people. Ogern roused that fear against me last night. Yet I do not think that he and Resad are afraid of me, though certainly they seek my death. Belert was kind, and he looked at me with sympathy. I cannot understand why he remained silent when I was sent to the grove.

The wolves hunt farther and farther away. Their calls grow fainter as the moon sets, but I dare not sleep. When dawn begins to light the east, I face the question that is more painful than my fear of Ogern and Resad and worse than my loneliness in this barrow.

Who is my mother?

Grenna carried me, a few days old, into the Vale of Enfert. She nursed me; her milk came in full enough after a few days of rest and good food. I slept beside her in the bedplace till I was old enough to sleep alone. Moren spoke often of watching me learn to walk by hanging on to her tunic as she worked about our homestead.

When the village children teased me about my language, my blue eyes and dark hair, my strange parents, I ran home weeping to Grenna. She would say, "Don't cry, lass. It's all right. You belong with us, and there is a place far away for the three of us. Someday we'll go. Don't mind the others; stay here with me awhile."

The first rays of morning sunlight catch the fortress and reflect off of something shiny—a watchman's spear, perhaps—atop the wall. So too the morning sun would warm our farm in Enfert before it touched the valley below us. I long to be there again, going about morning chores with my parents, sharing my breakfast bread with Cryner, and greeting Rol in his snug corner of our barn.

I rub at sudden tears and make myself concentrate on my situation now. It does no good to weep and long for childhood.

As the sun rises higher, the fortress gates open for the day, and boys drive livestock out to pasture. I watch and pray for the sight of a gray-haired woman hurrying in my direction.

A shaggy pony pulls a cart along the road that leads to the gate. The driver, cloaked against the morning chill, stands beside two tall baskets with something piled in them. Behind him two women with bundles atop their heads stride along at a brisk pace. Another cart just coming into view holds three children. Two adults walk beside the ox that draws it.

A steady stream of people and carts moves through the entrances. More traffic stretches out along the road. This must be market day at Dun Alyn.

I watch closely, but Ryamen does not come.

Something has happened to her. There is no other explanation. She would not abandon me otherwise. I think of her standing over me in the Oak Grove with the torch smoking beside her, her tears when she heard of Moren's death, and the warm hug she gave me in the barrow.

Could she be— I interrupt the thought. It is crazy. Grenna is my mother, and I won't think of anything else.

But Ryamen took a great risk to save me, and now she is in danger herself. I owe her my life! I cannot walk away to safety and leave her.

I tie my sling around my waist, pull on my vest, and pin the cloak close about me. I dare not be seen moving straight across the open meadow to the road, so I crouch low and hurry through the tall grass to the strip of woods and bramble bushes that borders the clearing. As I make my way through brush and trees to the road, I pick handfuls of late berries for breakfast.

People are still traveling toward the fortress. Before I step out into view, I pull even more of my tangled hair down over my face and drag the hood of the gray cloak forward.

I saunter along the edge of the road, munching the last of the berries and forcing myself to move slowly. A cart driver yells from behind, and I jump off onto the grass, where I stand and watch for a few minutes.

A group of young women is coming, and I step out in front of them. Soon enough they catch up to me, and by the time we've reached the first ring of the fortress, I'm in their midst. They are chattering so intently about some bit of gossip involving a sister of a friend that I don't think they even notice me. I look around at them as we walk. There are four, all about my age. None carries a bundle or basket, and I wonder what their business is at the fortress.

The sentries at the first entrance are playing a game with dice and stone markers. They glance up from time to time but find nothing to worry them in our group. The second entrance has no guards, and we proceed directly to the tall gateway that leads into the compound. Here the guards are watching closely. I shrink back as far as I can into my hood and try to stay between two of my new companions.

"Ho! You there." The shout comes from the watchman on our right. I stop, terrified, but make no answer. I feel a rough hand on my shoulder, and a push sends me through the gate to sprawl on the dirt inside. "Not you. Think I'd want a dirty wench with hair in her face?"

Peals of laughter greet this. I peer up through my curtain of hair as I scramble to my feet. The man who spoke has his arm around the woman who walked in beside me. She is laughing and pulling playfully at his beard. The other sentry is engaged in serious conversation with another of the young women.

I can guess what business my companions are about. I scurry away, trying to look as dirty and undesirable as possible. I don't care to be involved in those transactions.

I find a dim corner near the stables where I can see most of the area inside the ramparts. It was dark when I was here before, and I had no time to get my bearings. Dun Alyn is even larger than I thought.

A kitchen stretches along one side. Three hunting hounds wrestle over a bone near the door. Smoke rises from fires outside, and large ovens steam with morning baking. I'll come back here later; food is usually handed out at a fortress's kitchen door after the family and guests have eaten.

A blacksmith's forge and other work areas are near the stable. Family houses are grouped throughout the compound. I count twenty-three small homes from where I am standing, and there are more behind the stables. Well over two hundred people must live inside these walls.

The wide avenue leading to the Great Hall is packed with carts and baskets of produce. Women sit on low stools with woven cloth or skeins of wool and linen yarn spread out around them. Several crates of chickens add commotion and stray feathers. A metalworker unloads a display from his cart onto a bench.

An old woman walks through the press of people, holding up a stoppered gourd container and saying something I can't hear.

I would like to stroll about and look at the things for sale, but I have more important business. The sound of horses from the stables draws me.

I move to the back of a barn and peer in the door. Cormec would not have had time to get Rol to Dun Dreug. My horse must be in one of these barns. I can see no one inside. Perhaps I could . . .

Suddenly someone behind me speaks. "What's this?"

I turn to find a stable boy staring at me. His grin promises no good. I try a weak, slurred whine. "Is this where they keep the 'orses, sir?"

He looks pleased at the "sir." "Aye. And what you be wanting with the horses, girl?"

"Me brother promised me we'd see the big 'orses, but 'e's off with a lass."

This earns me a sly look. "I could show you the horses. And you'd be grateful, I reckon."

I'm not pleased with the turn the conversation is taking. "I don't know what you mean, sir. Are there really 'orses 'ere?"

He is beaming now. "Sure, lass. You come with me." He reaches for my arm. I try to shrug away. "Aw, now. I'll just lead you. It's a bit dark and hard to get around in there."

I pull my arm back and hug the cloak close.

His face hardens. "Let's see what's under that cloak. Be you worth bothering with?" He grabs a handful of gray wool and pulls.

I jerk loose and aim a hard kick. He doubles over and howls.

I back away quickly and scream, "Don't touch me. Me brother told me not to let anyone touch me. I'll tell 'im an' 'e'll be after you, 'e will." I turn and race back into the crowd in front of the stables.

The scent of food is stronger now. I inhale deeply. Berries are nourishing but not very filling. I would like a real meal. I move on toward the Great Hall with a few backward glances to be sure the stable boy is not following me. There is no sign of Ryamen in the crowd.

I wish I could throw back the cloak hood so I could see better, but I don't know who might recognize me. I stop to examine cloth spread out on the ground. The work is fine, with close, even weaving and skillful use of blue woad dye. I compliment the woman who sits beside it.

"Lovely work, lady."

She beams and smooths the piece with hands twisted from rheumatism. I think of the pain this piece of fabric has cost her.

A metalworker shows gold bracelets and circlets. I wonder how many can afford his wares. A young man is bargaining for a twisted-wire headpiece. I listen as the price is agreed on.

"A bag of oats from this harvest and two chickens, then. Though it's dear enough."

"A loss to me! How I'll make a living giving things away like this, I don't know."

"I'll get your oats and the fowl. Don't sell it to another, now."

"Aye, and I'd like to. Chickens are a nuisance. Mind you tie them well."

"And using my own thong, I suppose?"

"For the price I'm giving you, a bundle of thongs! And why you folk don't use coin, I don't know."

"It's mostly been melted down by metalworkers for overpriced jewelry." The buyer hurries away to get his part of the trade. Both men look pleased enough despite their complaints.

I can see where Moren came by the things he brought home from his trips. Did he walk through this same market disguised from those who would know him, or did Ryamen or someone else purchase what he wanted and take it out to him?

People are gathering by the kitchen door. As I move closer, I see the stable boy I met earlier, and I hurry away before he can see me. Back in the market area the crowd has begun to thin. I feel conspicuous now and look for a place to get out of sight while I decide where to look for Ryamen.

A clump of oaks stands against the ramparts and near a cluster of family houses. I weave my way between a cart of crated chickens and a woodworker's stack of stools and head across open ground toward the trees. This must be the main roadway, as it is rutted from cart and chariot wheels and strewn with fresh manure. I keep a close eye on where I step and so don't see the child in front of me until I bump into his back.

"Why don't you watch where you're going, wench?" It is not a child's voice. He turns, and I see a man's face, rough and bearded. I recover my balance and stare at him. He is no taller than a boy of eight or nine summers, but his head is large, almost normal adult size. I can't see his legs under the cloak he holds around himself, but I guess that they are short like his arms. He wears wide gold bracelets above child-size hands. An enameled brooch closes the cloak.

It is his face that holds my attention. His forehead is large and flat, with coarse, dark hair bushing up above it. His ears are little, and his thick neck goes straight down from his head without any curve at all. Deep folds around his eye sockets almost hide his eyes.

"Look at me, then. Look your fill. Stupid girl. Have you no manners?" He turns and stomps away.

I cringe at the anger in his voice. I've been staring rudely. I've never seen a dwarf before, though I've heard about them often. I call after him, "I'm sorry, sir. I was watching where I walked and did not see you."

He stops at my words and whirls around. His eyes are dark, and they fix on my face with a frightening intensity. I hold my breath as he moves back to stand close to me. I realize that I forgot my disguise and spoke without the whine.

He reaches up with both hands and parts my hair so he can see my face. I want to run away, but I am frozen to the spot. The noise of the market dims in my ears, and I cannot measure the time we two spend, silent and unmoving, staring at each other.

When he speaks, the anger is gone from his voice. "They told me true. You could be the lady herself."

I gulp and swallow down the dryness in my throat. "Which lady, sir? Who do people mistake me for?"

He looks past me, and I hear horses bearing down on us. He drops my hair over my face and growls, "Don't turn around."

The voice behind me is familiar. "Well, Spusscio, what do you have? A wench, it seems." Resad's laugh mingles with another man's.

"Aye," the dwarf says, "if we can agree on a price."

"She can't be worth much. I saw her come in with the others, and the worst of the lot, she looks."

"Well, she values herself highly enough." Spusscio has taken hold of my arm. I'm surprised at the strength in the little hand.

"Here. I'm glad to help out in a good cause." Two coins fall into the dirt at our feet.

"Thank you, Resad. Your generosity is exceeded only by your kind heart." There is a bitter edge to my companion's voice. He jerks me to his side and, at the same time, turns me so that my face is away from the horsemen as they ride by. Their laughter mixes with the dirt their horses churn up.

The dwarf doesn't release my arm until he has tugged me across the roadway to the cluster of oaks. Once we are inside their shelter, he lets me go. I look around for someplace to get away from him.

"Oh, lass, I won't hurt you. I apologize for the rough words, but that's what Resad understands." His voice is courteous, and I sense a genuine warmth.

"What do you plan to do with me?"

He laughs. "If you're the fighter I heard you were, I probably couldn't do anything with you. With your permission, I'd like to take you to Belert. He will be relieved to see that you are well."

I think back to the Great Hall, to Belert's face when he spoke with me, to his expression when Ogern sent me to the Oak Grove. If I am to find Ryamen, I need help, and I cannot stay out here where everyone can see me. "Gladly," I say.

Spusscio sets a quick pace across the compound to one of the dwelling places behind the Great Hall. When we enter the dim interior, I find that it is larger than it looked from across the grounds. We move to a wooden door set in a wicker partition. I can see four other doors around the central hearth.

Spusscio points to the door to our right. "That is the chief's chamber. No one lives in this house now except the two of us." He shoves the door in front of me open. "You can stay in here."

I step inside as he opens shutters to let daylight in. The room is luxurious. It is almost as large as our entire house in the West. The sleeping ledge is wide, with a thick layer of soft skins over the straw. There is a lovely carved larchwood box under the window and other boxes and baskets on shelves along one side of the space. Woven hangings cover the wicker on two walls. The room has its own small hearth in the center, and a table with two benches is nearby. A gaming board with stone pieces sits on the table, waiting, it seems, for the room's occupant to return.

Spusscio watches me with a curious look. "Do you like this room?" he asks.

"It is lovely. I've never been in such a fine place." I remove Ryamen's cloak and lay it on the bed. I would like to lie down on those soft skins and sleep the rest of the day away. "But this is someone else's room. Is it all right for me to be here?"

"She doesn't need it now." His voice is sad.

I remember the story of Cara and Miquain. "Surely I shouldn't be in here."

"It is safe for you."

"Will the chief mind?"

"No, he'll understand why I've put you here. I'll come for you when he returns from dinner."

"Is there . . ." I hesitate. It is rude for a guest to ask

for things, I know. And I have no idea what my status is. I may be a prisoner here. Still, the mention of dinner brings sharp hunger pangs. "Might I have something to eat?"

"I'm sorry, lady. Stumbling into you like that has driven sensible thoughts from my mind. I will bring you food at once." He moves to the door, then turns. "And would you like to wash?"

"Oh, please. I've been in a cave and a cage and a barrow. I'm so dirty I don't even feel human."

He smiles. "Well, there are those who say you aren't human."

I sigh. "I hope you'll explain that."

"When you've washed and dined, we will sit with Belert and talk. We have much to ask you, and we'll try to answer your questions." He goes out and closes the door firmly behind him.

I walk around the chamber, admiring things. There is a mirror on the top shelf, and I hold it to the light. My face is filthy, my hair straggles around it, and my tunic is torn and bloody at the shoulder. The wound on my forehead looks healed. If I can wash away the dried blood and dirt, it will hardly show. I put the mirror back and look down at my legs. My trousers and boots are caked with mud, and my tunic is almost as bad.

There is a noise outside the entrance. Spusscio speaks quietly. "Can you open the door?"

He brings a kettle of steaming water and a large basin and sets them on the floor. "I'll be back with cold water. I don't want the servants to know you are here, so I'll get it myself."

When he returns, he carries a bucket of cold water with a ladle in it and a bundle of scrubbing twigs wrapped in a linen towel. He sets the cold water beside the basin and puts the towel and twigs on the table. "I'll get the fire going for you."

He leaves for a moment and returns with a handful of blazing twigs. After he has lit the kindling and laid on logs from a pile in the corner, he straightens up and gestures toward the larchwood box and the containers on the shelves. "You will find clean clothes in those."

When the door shuts behind Spusscio, I strip off my dirty things and step into the basin. I dip the ladle first into the cold water, then the hot, and pour the mixture over my body. When I'm wet enough, I scrub the soapwort twigs into a lather on my skin and rinse with more clear, warm water.

The basin is full long before I'm finished. I peer out the window and see nothing but the back rampart wall and a clump of shrubs. I dump the dirty water over the bushes and return to my bath. I savor the feel of clean water coursing over my skin with each ladleful. Finally, with both kettle and bucket empty, I rub myself dry with the strip of linen.

The dwarf seemed certain I could borrow clean clothes, but I hesitate before the box. At last I lift the lid. I find a clean undershift and pull it on thankfully. The fresh linen is finely woven and feels smooth against my body. I lift a tunic and see a familiar fabric under it.

I packed my girdle in my saddle bundle at Dun Dreug. It should be with Rol in the stable—if he is still there. It could not be here, deep in someone else's storage chest, but what is this?

I pull the embroidered cloth out of the chest and smooth the fabric with my hand, feeling the silky raised needlework. The pattern is similar to mine, but there are differences. Though the colors are alike, the flowers are not the same. There is a stain on the front of this one, and the ties are frayed. I study it carefully; it is soft with wear. I have worn mine only a few times.

I feel a shiver down my body as I hold the piece. It's not really so strange that something Moren brought me from Dun Alyn looks like another piece of fabric here, but I have an eerie feeling about it.

I look through the clothes and find a woolen dress in a beautiful shade of green. I pull it over my head and tie it with the girdle. There are slippers on one of the shelves, and I tug them on, then attack my hair with a sturdy bone comb.

When I hear Spusscio at the door again, I hurry to help him in. He has a large bread trencher piled with slices of beef and root vegetables in one hand and balances a small loaf of wheat bread on a flagon of ale with the other. He places the lot on the table and puts the dirk from his belt beside the food.

I am so hungry I barely remember to thank him

before I start eating. He lifts the basin of dirty water but stands staring at me instead of leaving.

I swallow a large chunk of beef and ask, "What's wrong? I'm sorry if my manners offend you. I haven't had good food for days."

He shakes his head. "You could be Miquain. You must be Miquain, though I know you are not."

I remember the bard's story. "Miquain? Cara and Belert's daughter?"

"Aye. You look just like her."

I look around. "Is this her room?"

He nods.

I swallow some of the ale. "Perhaps I should not have put on her clothes." I look with distaste toward the pile of soiled things I've removed.

"I will tell him I told you to. He won't mind." He balances the basin and moves to the door. I rise to open it, then close it tightly after him.

I finish the meat and vegetables and, when the loaf of fine wheat bread is gone, even eat most of the coarse, crusty trencher. I am swallowing the last of the ale when the door bursts open.

Chief Belert steps into the room.

CHAPTER 11

I LEAP TO MY FEET, WIPING AT MY GREASY MOUTH AND hands with the linen towel left from my bath.

He stands without moving, staring at me. Finally he speaks in a soft voice. "Miquain? Is it you, then?"

The look on his face moves me to tears. I want at this moment to be Miquain, to do anything or be anyone that might bring comfort to this tragic man. But I can only speak as gently as possible. "I'm sorry to startle you, sir. I am not Miquain."

"You are not Miquain?" He looks old, bewildered.

I cannot check my tears. I swipe at my face with the towel. "I am Ilena. Remember? I was in the hall three nights ago."

He makes an effort to recover himself. "Yes. Ogern sent you to the grove. He said wolves broke in and took you."

"I escaped from the wolves." I am still not ready to say Ryamen's name.

"Why are you in Miquain's room?" He does not sound angry, just deeply sorrowful.

"I brought her here, Belert." Spusscio speaks from behind him. "I meant to warn you, but I missed you in the hall."

"She is not Miquain." This time he sounds resigned.

"No. She is not. I think we must decide who she is."

"Yes. Yes, certainly." Belert looks for a place to sit.

Spusscio brings us more ale and a large stack of sweet cakes. He hands them to me and motions toward the door. "We should go into your quarters, sir. If anyone comes they will not be surprised to hear voices in there."

"Yes." Belert looks around Miquain's room slowly. He notices my clothes and the open box on the floor.

I start to say something but catch Spusscio's eye. He shakes his head, and I remain silent.

I follow the chief into his chamber. Spusscio comes behind, carrying the kettle and bucket with the towel and limp soapstone twigs inside. He stacks them by the door.

This chamber is much larger than Miquain's. There are thick hangings over all the walls, and two windows look out on the ramparts. The bedplace is wide and richly appointed. A large table with benches enough for several people stands near the hearth. Boxes and baskets sit about the room and on the shelves. A shield much like the one I carried from Enfert stands in a corner with a bundle of spears. A sword in a gold-trimmed scabbard leans in another corner, its chape nestled into a groove between floor stones.

Belert sits at the table and leans his head in his hands. Spusscio stirs the smoldering fire to life. A light rain has begun to fall, and I can see dark clouds above the ramparts. I place the food and drink on the large table and look around for something to wipe the honey off my fingers. Spusscio sees my problem and gets me the linen towel from the bucket.

When both of us are settled, Belert looks up and speaks. "Now, Spusscio, how do we have Ilena here in this place?"

"She stumbled over me on the grounds. I recognized her from the description I'd been given and thought this the safest place for her."

"Does anyone know you brought her here?"

"I don't think so. Resad spoke to us outside, but Ilena's face was hidden. He'd seen her enter with those girls from Leven Dale and assumed I was bargaining for her favors." Spusscio turns to me. "I apologize again, lady, for so insulting you."

I laugh. "It was quick thinking. I would rather risk my reputation than my life. I'd already been rejected by the sentries and fought my way free of a stable boy. I didn't realize what kind of women I was joining when I walked in with that group."

Belert says, "Probably the safest disguise you could have managed. Now, tell us how you freed yourself in the grove." He is sitting straight now, and his voice has the sound of authority. He must have recovered from the surge of grief my appearance caused.

I do not answer him. I cannot bring myself to lie to these two. Still, I will not name Ryamen.

The chief seems to understand my dilemma. "You are loyal to whoever helped you. I admire that. I would have come to your aid that night, but Ogern drugged my ale. I could not think clearly or speak."

"Yes," Spusscio says, "I heard the story yesterday when I returned from a journey. I tried to wake you but it was impossible, so I hurried alone to the grove. I found Ogern and Resad there puzzling over the empty cage."

I remain silent.

Spusscio gets up. "I think I can answer your question, Belert." He leaves the room and returns with Ryamen's cloak, folded as I left it with the brooch pinned on top. He hands it to Belert.

The chief studies the brooch. He traces the swirls with his finger. "There is no doubt, is there?"

Spusscio shakes his head. Both look at me. Belert speaks. "My wife gave this brooch to Ryamen. She would not have parted with it lightly."

There is no point in staying quiet. "She gave me the cloak to keep me warm until she returned, but she never came back."

"She released you from the cage, then?" Belert asks.

I rub the gouge in my shoulder and think back to the wolves and my fear. "Yes. She drove away the wolves too, and took me to a barrow of the old ones."

Spusscio says, "There was a dead wolf in the pen. Did you kill it?"

I nod. I can still feel the coarse fur under my hands and smell the sharp animal scent.

"I will try to find out what has happened to Ryamen," Spusscio says.

Belert settles on the bench with his back against the wall. "Now, Ilena, will you tell us about yourself?"

I begin with my childhood in the Vale of Enfert. When I speak of the journeys Moren made every year, both men have questions. "What time of year did he come?" "What did he bring back?" "What did he say?" "Did he mention names?" I answer the best I can, but as I explain, he and Grenna took care that I not overhear their conversations about his trips.

When I tell about Moren's last days, Belert wipes his eyes. "He was my close friend as well as my wife's brother." He falls silent at the look on my face.

"Moren was your wife's brother?"

He nods. "I thought you knew. Didn't Moren tell you anything about your lineage?"

"No," I say, "though it was clear that we were different from others in the valley. Moren knew everything about defense and warfare. Both my parents told stories about fortresses and great halls that they had visited, and Moren spoke of battles and heroes. He said our people's women often led war bands, and he trained me to be a warrior."

Spusscio laughs. "You could not have a better reference than that, Ilena. Moren was the greatest military expert in the North. Many would say in Britain."

I stare into the fire for a time, trying to grasp this new information. At last I stand to stretch my legs and try to clear my head. Belert and Spusscio are silent while I walk to the window and look out into the dreary evening sky. When I turn around, Belert speaks.

"I know you are tired, Ilena, but we need to ask you more questions."

I nod. "I understand. I'll try to help, but I can't make any sense of it."

"Begin by telling us about your journey, especially about the battle." His eyes are steady on my face. I feel that he is seeing me now and not Miquain.

I tell of meeting Durant and of Chief Perr's hospitality. I describe the trip over the mountains with Gola and Cochan and my trip alone down the mountain and across the valley. When I say, "The group of painted ones was waiting for me in the clearing," Spusscio interrupts me.

"Painted? Where? On their faces?"

"Tattoos on the face," I answer. "And they had the high cheekbones of the northern ones. Many at Dun Dreug had tattoos on their arms and shoulders, but these were different."

Spusscio nods. "Aye. That would fit. Cormec said

they were from beyond Red Mountain. It is strange that they chose to attack you. They do not take slaves, and one horse would not tempt them."

"There was another person there," I say.

"You tried to tell me something in the hall," Belert says. "Was that it?"

"Yes. Ogern kept me from speaking."

"I am sorry. If the drugged ale had not weakened me, I could have shouted him down and kept control of the hall."

I shake my head. "Resad kept starting calls for my death. He stirred everyone up. And"—I pause for a moment—"Resad was the other person at the fork in the trail."

The two sit staring at me for several minutes. Then Belert turns to Spusscio. "You are right. Ogern and Resad have been hard at work."

The dwarf says, "I take no joy in being right, Belert. In this case I would like to be wrong."

"Spusscio has been telling me for some time that Ogern is behind the tragedies that have overtaken Dun Alyn. I refused to believe him, but if they will attempt to kill you, perhaps . . ." The chief's voice trails off.

"Perhaps they plotted the attack on Dun Alyn," Spusscio finishes.

Belert sighs. "His niece and"—his voice breaks on the word—"Miquain."

Spusscio speaks in a weary voice. "Ogern has become more and more convinced that he must hold the old ways firm against the new religion. It is a crusade for him. A man is not rational when he lets one thought blind him to everything else."

"Their own uncle." Belert's voice is low and harsh.

"I fear so, Belert."

"I will avenge their deaths." The look in his eyes is frightening. "But first I must hold Dun Alyn against Ogern's claim for his granddaughter."

Spusscio points to me. "Ilena is the true heir."

I stare back at him with my mouth open. Heir to Dun Alyn? It is a crazy thought.

Belert watches me in silence for a time before he speaks. "Certainly! You are Cara's niece."

"But if I am not Grenna's daughter . . . ?"

"Ogern was right about Grenna," Belert says. "Ryamen said that she could have no more children. That deepened her grief over the infant's death."

"But midwives have been wrong," Spusscio turns to me. "Do you know when Moren and Grenna arrived at the Vale of Enfert?"

"What do you mean?" Belert asked.

"If Ryamen was wrong, Grenna could have borne another child while they lived somewhere else," Spusscio said. "Ilena would be Miquain's cousin and a year or two younger."

"I know the story told in the vale about us," I say. "It begins, 'They came at the end of the long winter.' "

Spusscio sighs, and Belert's face falls.

"Is that a problem?" I ask.

"Yes," Spusscio replies. "It was the end of the long winter when Grenna's child was born; the little boy lived only a day. And so you cannot be Grenna's daughter."

I have feared as much since I asked Ryamen about my name, but I am not ready to talk about it with others. "Grenna is the only mother I've known," I say.

Belert says, "We do not know the truth, Ilena. Grenna was certainly your true mother, though another may have borne you. The important thing for our purpose is that you are Moren's daughter. And no one who sees you can doubt that relationship. You look like him."

Spusscio says, "As Moren's daughter, Ilena is granddaughter to Gwlech and Fergus just as Miquain was."

"What did Moren tell you before he died?" Belert asks.

I think back to the house on the slope of the Vale of Enfert, to the time when Moren lay ill. I try to remember every word, every pause. "He said, 'We planned to go together but Grenna . . .' He stopped there. Then he said, 'It is time, we must go.' "

"Is that all?" Spusscio asks.

"He said, 'Go to Dun Alyn. Find Ryamen.' " My eyes are wet with the recollection, but my throat is dry from speaking. I raise my flagon and sip the last drops of ale. I can hardly stay awake now that I'm warm and fed.

Belert stares out the window. At last he turns to us.

"We must decide how to move against Ogern. And"—he smiles at me—"we must let Ilena rest soon."

"Ogern will challenge us. He has been planning this for a long time," Spusscio says.

"Yes," Belert agrees. "And he has allies. The band that struck the fortress was well prepared, as was the one at the fork with Resad." He turns to me and speaks in a solemn voice. "How say you, Ilena? Are you willing to fight for Dun Alyn?"

I remember the hostility in the Great Hall, the chants for my death, the blazing hatred in Ogern's eyes. I survived Resad's ambush only because Dun Alyn's war band arrived when it did. And the terrors of the cage in the Oak Grove! If Ryamen had not come to my aid . . .

Moren traveled here year after year, always returning to the West to help Grenna raise me. They spoke of this life, trained me to be a warrior, taught me the stories and customs of Dun Alyn. I know how they would advise me.

"Yes," I say. "I will fight for Dun Alyn."

Belert looks me full in the eyes from across the table. "It may not be a successful battle. Ogern has raised a following. I do not know how many will remain loyal to me."

I hear his words, but I respond to the look in his eyes. Something compelling calls me to follow this man. "My destiny is in this place. I am sure of that."

"Spoken like Moren's daughter," Spusscio says.

"If you are certain," the chief says. He watches me closely for a few moments. Then he continues. "Good. Now Spusscio and I will consider how to proceed, and you should rest."

"Thank you," I answer, "but I must search for Ryamen. There is some reason she didn't come back for me."

Spusscio says, "You stay out of sight. I'll look for Ryamen." He grins, and his deep-set eyes twinkle. "We'll wake you for supper."

The bed in Miquain's chamber is even more comfortable than it looks. Spusscio has started a fire in the hearth, and rain splashes gently on leaves outside the window. I spend a very short time wondering what it would be like to live in such luxury before sleep forces my eyes shut.

I awaken to Spusscio's voice. "Ilena. Wake up. I've brought us supper. It's in Belert's room."

I'm surprised to find myself hungry again. Spusscio has set a kettle of stew and a pile of wheat loaves beside the ale on the table. The fire burns brightly, and the room's shutters have been closed against a damp wind off the sea.

Belert takes a dirk from a shelf and hands it to me. "Keep this. I noticed you don't have one."

"Thank you. They took mine at the Oak Grove." I lay the knife on the table before me. The blade is fine steel, honed to a keen edge. The handle is bone, intricately carved in scrolls and circles that swirl into an animal figure. The creature's snout is a blunt square that forms the end of the hilt.

Neither man has mentioned Ryamen. I'm almost afraid to ask the question on my mind, but I must know. "Did you find Ryamen?"

They exchange glances, and I know the news is bad. Finally Spusscio speaks. "I went to her house. There is no sign of her. The hearth is cold, and the plants piled on her table are wilted."

"I spoke to one who lives near her. He said he hasn't seen her since yesterday morning," Belert adds.

Suddenly my hunger vanishes. The warmth in her voice when she spoke to me, the affection in her eyes, her concern for my safety have all made Ryamen important to me.

"I will search tomorrow," I say.

"No, lass," Belert says. "There is something else you must do tomorrow. I will not forget Ryamen; she is my friend too. I can go places in the fortress and outside that you cannot. Trust me. I will not give up."

"Eat now, Ilena," Spusscio says. "I know you are hungry. It takes more than one meal to make up for days on short rations." He settles across the table from me and stabs his dirk into a piece of pork.

Belert takes a stool from the corner and sits at the end of the table. He ladles out a small serving of stew and stares down at it.

I break off a piece of bread and scoop up sauce and vegetables from the portion Spusscio has placed in front of me. My appetite returns, and I eat in silence for a few minutes before I speak. "You said there was something I must do tomorrow. What is it? And where do I sleep?"

Spusscio answers, "You can spend tonight in Miquain's room. We'll bank the fire low, and you can keep the door closed. No one will be back here." He turns to Belert. "Do you want to tell her your plan?"

Belert scoops up a morsel of stew and chews for a while. Then he swallows a draught of ale and says, "We think we can get you out of the fortress tomorrow if you don't mind continuing the masquerade you began this morning."

I nod. "I can do that, though I look a good deal cleaner now."

Belert laughs. "It won't show under the cloak. Spusscio will ride out with you behind him. He'll pretend he is taking you home after spending the night with him."

"And what do I do when I get outside the fortress?"

"Let me explain," Belert says. "I do not have the authority to lead Dun Alyn now that my wife and daughter are no longer with us." His voice falters on the last words, but he draws a deep breath and continues. "As Moren's daughter, you are the heir."

"How do I make that claim?" I ask.

"That is the problem," Spussico says. "If you walk openly into the Great Hall, Ogern will continue his superstitious tirades about spirits. He is the Druid, and many recognize his religious leadership."

"And some who claim the new religion still hold enough of the old beliefs to avoid angering Ogern or his gods," Belert adds. "I fear for your safety. He and Resad have made two attempts on your life. I want you away from here until I feel sure we can protect you."

"I said I would fight for Dun Alyn," I say. "I do not propose to begin by running away."

Belert smiles. "Moren has taught you well. I have new hope for Dun Alyn because of you, Ilena."

"But," Spusscio says, "getting you killed will not advance our cause. Hear Belert out."

I scrape the last of the stew from my trencher and eye the kettle. Spusscio ladles more meat and gravy onto the bread. Belert refills our flagons from the cauldron and settles down on his bench.

The chief says, "We may not have enough warriors to hold if Ogern opposes us. I don't know how many will stand with me against him. We must make a claim for you as heir and at the same time have a strong show of force so all who want to support me know it is safe to do so."

"Who, then, are your allies?" I ask.

"Perr of Dreug and others who ride with Arthur will come to my aid. They know well that Ogern opposes Arthur and would open Dun Alyn to his enemies. Will you ride to Dreug and plead our cause?"

"Of course." I hope I sound brave. "Is my horse still in the stables?"

"Yes," Spusscio says, "the stablemaster has him in a large stall by himself. We plan to get him for you."

"If our ruse works," Belert says.

"Will you come to Dreug too?" I ask him. "You also would be safer there."

The chief shakes his head. "I have asked Spusscio to go with you. I would like to go myself, but I think it wiser to stay here in the fortress."

I understand. "It would be a mistake to let Ogern have full control."

Spusscio says, "We must make an early start. Can you be ready to ride at daylight?"

"Of course," I answer. I finish my ale, say my good-nights, and go to Miquain's room.

Her bed is as soft and inviting as it was before. The strain of the past days has caught up with me. I'm still tired despite my long nap, and the whirl of new ideas makes a fog in my mind. The thoughts about my place as Dun Alyn's chief seem so remote I can't grasp them.

I think of Grenna. How I want to hear her voice, to feel her hand stroke my hair like she used to. The tears fall freely for a time until I force myself to think of something else.

Will I see Durant at Dun Dreug? Surely he could not have completed his business there and moved on so quickly. It has been three days since I left him, but I can still feel the clasp of his hand on my arm when we said goodbye.

At last my mind stops churning, and I relax. I can hear the murmur of Belert's and Spusscio's voices through the wicker wall as I go to sleep.

CHAPTER 12

MORNING IS BRIGHT AND CLEAR. I DRESS QUICKLY IN clean traveling clothes. There is a fine pair of boots on one of the shelves. I look from them to my stiff, mud-caked pair. I pull on Miquain's and find them a comfortable fit. I take time to plait my hair and hope that my helmet is still with Rol's gear. I brush the dried mud off my heavy war vest before putting it on, and I carry Ryamen's cloak with me.

Next door there are warm ale and loaves for breakfast. Belert is kneeling beside a large storage box, rummaging in the contents.

He glances around as I come in. "Good, you have found some clothes." He turns back to the box and continues moving things about. "I'm looking for Cara's old helmet. I can't find it."

"Mine was on Rol's saddle," I say. "It should still be there." I reach out for extra bread to take with us.

Spusscio laughs. "Ilena, I have food enough for three or four in my pack."

Belert closes the box and joins us at the table. "Take a loaf or two with you anyway. It will add to your disguise as a poor country girl."

"A fine threesome we are," Spusscio says. "A dwarf, a madman, and a hungry doxy."

"Aye," Belert agrees. "Ogern started the talk that I had lost my mind with grief. We'll use it against him this morning."

"You'll keep out of his way while we're gone?" Spusscio asks. "I don't like to leave you unguarded."

"I'll wander about, mumbling. That way I can search for Ryamen," Belert says. "Your job is to protect Ilena. She is more important to Dun Alyn than I am."

Spusscio nods, but I can see the worry in his eyes when he looks at his chief.

I pull the hood of Ryamen's cloak far forward as we leave the house. I've left some of my hair out of the plait, and I drag it over my face with one hand as we walk. With the other I clutch two loaves of wheat bread.

At the stables there is a comfortable noise of horses stamping and chewing. We enter at one end of a long barn, and I can hear a commotion at the far end.

"Steady, fellow." There is a snort and the sound of hooves hitting wood. Then I hear a whinny that I recognize.

"Rol," I whisper. "That's my horse."

Spusscio pushes me behind him, and I scuttle along at his heels, peering out through my hair.

Belert strides ahead of us and speaks. "What's this? I intend to ride this animal today."

I recognize the voice that answers him. "I'm sorry, sir. I don't think anyone can ride this beast."

"Stand aside, Cormec." Belert says. "I don't intend to have a good horse like this in the stables without trying him out."

"I've been trying to harness him for two days. He won't let me close."

"Well, if he can't be ridden, we'll dispose of him." Belert sounds much different from the thoughtful man I've come to know; he is waving his sword around wildly now.

Cormec's voice takes on a cautious, almost pleading tone. "Let me help you back to your quarters. You don't seem well."

"Well? I'm well! I'm going to ride this horse and see if it comes from the spirit world. Maybe it'll take me to my ladies. Stand aside, Cormec."

I steal a look over Spusscio's shoulder. Rol is calm now; he has sensed my presence and is staring in my direction.

Cormec is blocking the stall entrance. "I cannot let you near this horse."

Belert waves his sword again. "Get out of this stable. I am chief here, and I order you out. I'll ride this animal or be rid of it."

"Sir, I beg you. Reconsider. I'm under oath to protect you, but also to care for this horse."

"How could you be under oath to a horse? Spusscio, hear that. Cormec thinks he is under oath to a horse." Belert laughs wildly.

Cormec says, "My chief, I fear you are ill. Let me take you back to your quarters. Or let me saddle your own fine horse for you. I'll accompany you if you wish to ride."

"I'll ride this horse!" Belert says.

Cormec looks to Spusscio. "Will you reason with him? You can see he is not himself."

Spusscio says, "He has not been himself for some time. He insists he will ride this horse. Let me saddle it for him."

Cormec stays in front of the stall gate. "I swore an oath to the young lady that I would care for this horse and deliver it to Dun Dreug for her. I intend to do that. There is dishonor enough on Dun Alyn for her death. I'll not betray her again."

Belert is silent for a moment. Then he sheathes his sword and speaks quietly, without the ring of madness. "Cormec, are you questioning Ogern's orders?"

"Aye. And yours also. You were in that hall. Now, come into this stall if you will, but only over my body."

I push past Spusscio. "Cormec, I thank you for your

loyalty to me." I shove the hood back and brush the hair off my face.

He stares for a long moment; then a broad smile creases his face. "Lady! You are not dead, then."

"No, but I need to get Rol out of here."

There is a noise at the stable entrance. I can hear voices, one of them that of the stable boy I met yesterday. I pull my hood back on and duck my head.

Cormec steps away from the stall gate and speaks to Belert. "If you wish to ride this animal, I ask only that you be careful." In a low voice he adds, "Dun Alyn needs you."

Belert reaches out a hand to Cormec's shoulder and speaks softly. "Thank you, and Dun Alyn needs you, too." In a louder voice he says, "Spusscio! Help me with this beast. And bring that wench in with you. Maybe she can charm a horse the way she's charmed you."

When I step past Cormec, he smiles and nods to me before he turns away. I clasp Rol around his neck and lean my face against his warm skin. He nuzzles my shoulder and whinnies softly.

He stands quietly as long as I am near his head. Belert soon has him ready to go. He is careful to put my sword and helmet in their places; and then he lashes my pack behind the saddle. He inspects the long fighting lances and the bag of casting spears before he fastens them to the harness. Rol calmly follows me out of the stable while Spusscio gets his mount.

We are at the gates when they open for the day. I

ride behind Spusscio on his black mare. Belert comes after us so that Rol has me clearly in view. I have my head down over the loaves, and the hood falls forward almost to Spusscio's back. Through the curtain of hair, I can see the two sentries look at me and exchange amused glances.

One of them speaks. "A fine horse you're riding, sir."

"Aye," Belert says. "Thought I'd try out the horse a spirit girl rode."

"Out for a day of hunting, then?" the other asks.

"Perhaps. If anything wants to be hunted. First I'll escort Spusscio here while he takes his new friend home."

The sound of men's laughter follows us. I feel a sharp pang of sympathy for women who have no protection against men's contempt.

We move along at a steady pace until we reach forest cover. Spusscio turns off onto a faint trail that takes us to a secluded glade. I slide off of Spusscio's horse and hold Rol's bridle while Belert dismounts.

"Do you think we'll meet anyone from Dun Alyn?" I ask.

"No," Belert says. "I know of no one out last night, and we are ahead of everyone this morning. If you keep a good pace, you'll not be seen."

"How will you get back without a horse?" I ask.

He smiles. "I'll nap awhile here and then smear some dirt on myself. I'll limp back along the road this afternoon and say the horse threw me."

"And I, of course, have followed the horse to bring it back," adds Spusscio.

"Now, Ilena," Belert says in a solemn voice, "be careful. I don't want to lose you, too."

"I will," I say, "and we should return with help in four or five days."

"Go now, and Godspeed."

When we turn onto the road again, I can see him watching from the glade. I raise my hand and he gives an answering wave.

Spusscio sets a brisk pace on the level trail. He sits the black mare well, and it takes a second look to notice that he is not as large as other men. I realize that the distress I felt when I met him has vanished. He is just Spusscio now and not at all the odd creature I thought him at first.

The first ascent is an easy one. We stop only long enough to look back over the valley from the outcrop. I remember Cochan's thick arm pointing out my trail. Could that have been only three days ago?

A faint haze of smoke from the direction of Dun Alyn is all we can see of the fortress. Spusscio watches the trail behind us for a time. He sounds relieved when he speaks. "Looks like we're away safely."

"Will there be questions when you don't return?"

"Probably not. Few notice when a dwarf comes and goes. I keep myself out of sight. That has served Belert well as Ogern plots his mischief."

We push on to the summit, where we stop to look

around again. There is still no sign of anyone else on the mountain. It is well past noon, but Spusscio wants to keep moving.

"Can you eat and walk?" He hands me meat strips from his pack.

I pull the loaves I carried out of Dun Alyn from my pack and give him one. As a taskmaster, Spusscio is a match for Cochan. At this rate we will make Dun Dreug by nightfall tomorrow.

We stop for the night far down the west slope. I manage to stay awake long enough to help Spusscio tend the horses, and I fall asleep thinking of the comfortable bed at Dun Alyn.

The next morning finds us moving through a boulder field soon after sunrise. I have all I can do to keep up with Spusscio. He was still stirring about the horses when I went to sleep, and I heard him up long before me this morning. Yet he seems tireless as he hurries us along.

Our rest stop at the base of the next ascent is short, and we reach the second summit shortly after noon. Below us I see the stream that we will follow westward. A cloud of smoke on the horizon marks Dun Dreug. It is an easy route once we get down the mountainside, but I fear we cannot reach the gates before the time of lighting torches.

Once on level ground we lead the horses to the streamside to drink while we fill our waterskins. The sun is low in the west.

"We'll walk awhile yet," Spusscio says. "The horses are tired."

I nod. I'm tired too, but the trail is easy here.

"I hope Arthur's people are at Dun Dreug," Spusscio says. "I heard there was to be a gathering of those in the North at this time."

The thought of Durant makes me smile. I am eager to see him again. I can still see the look on his face when we said farewell. A warm flush moves through my body when I think of greeting him again. I remember how Fiona looked when she spoke of meeting her young man and wonder if I have the same bright eyes and pink cheeks.

The sun has slipped below the horizon, leaving red streaks across the darkening sky. The three-quarter moon, already risen above the mountains behind us, promises enough light to travel. Rol follows Spusscio's mare without my guidance. I walk close beside him.

Heir to Dun Alyn! The phrase has echoed in my mind since Spusscio first said it. It is so unbelievable I cannot even focus on it; my mind refuses to take the thought seriously. I understand that Belert can keep control of Dun Alyn if his people believe that I am the real heir, but I don't see how it could be true. And even more than I want to help Belert or to stay at Dun Alyn, I want to know my proper place.

Why did Moren and Grenna keep me in the West, away from everyone they knew? I had hoped to find answers at Dun Alyn, but each day brings more confusion.

Spusscio mounts his mare and looks back to me. I pull my thoughts to our present situation and swing onto Rol's back. It feels good to ride again, but we keep the animals at an easy gait. I can see moonlight gleaming on a lake, so we must be near Dun Dreug. There is a sharp scent of wood smoke on the evening breeze, and I fancy I can smell food cooking.

Spusscio turns onto the track that leads upward and waits for me to ride beside him. When we move out of tree cover, I hear the notes of a trumpet from somewhere high on the ramparts. There is a clink of metal ahead of us, and three sentries step out onto the path through the first entrance.

"Who approaches?"

I look to Spusscio and see that he is watching me. I gulp and say, "Ilena. Ilena of . . . of Dun Alyn. And my companion, Spusscio."

A sentry thrusts a torch into our faces.

Another speaks. "Aye. That's the lady Ilena. She is friend to Durant."

The man with the torch says, "Follow me." The others move aside and let us by.

At the second entrance we are scrutinized again, and another guard with a torch joins our escort. When we reach the main gate, Spusscio is riding a few paces behind me, and the two sentries walk beside

Rol's head. The trumpet sounds again. They must recognize me in the torchlight because the gates swing open.

A large man on horseback blocks our passage through the entrance. The torches move closer to him, and I recognize Cochan.

"Well met, Cochan," I say.

He nods to me. "Well met, Lady Ilena. Chief Perr is in council in the Great Hall." As he speaks, he peers behind me where Spusscio sits in deep shadows cast by the gates.

"Well met, Cochan." There is laughter in my companion's voice.

"Spusscio!" Cochan moves his horse around me and reaches out a hand in greeting. "I thought you had been killed by the painted ones long ago. I've heard nothing from you."

Spusscio replies, "And you! How have you managed to live so long with half the Northmen after your head?"

I move Rol farther into the compound, and the two of them, still exchanging friendly insults, follow me to the Great Hall.

Elban is at the door. "My lady! It is good to see you again. Chief Perr is unable to greet you now, but I'll find Gola to take you to your quarters."

"I need—" I start to protest, but Spusscio interrupts me.

"Tell Chief Perr that Ilena of Dun Alyn requires immediate counsel." There is a note of authority in his voice that I haven't heard before.

Elban looks from Spusscio back to me and nods. "Certainly, lady." He hurries into the hall.

"Ilena! Ilena, is that you?" It is Gola's voice.

"You said you missed her," Cochan booms. "I fetched her for you."

Gola laughs. She takes Rol's bridle and reaches an arm up to help me dismount. "I'm glad to see you well, lady. Shall I take your things to the women's quarters?"

"Please, Gola." I hand Rol's reins to a boy who has appeared from the direction of the stables.

Spusscio speaks from behind me. "See that these horses are rubbed down well and fed extra rations. They've had a hard trip."

Cochan says, "I'll make sure of it, Spusscio. And I'll put your things in the men's quarters for you."

Elban speaks from the doorway. "Perr asks me to bring you to him."

Five people are gathered at a table by the fire in Dun Dreug's Great Hall. Two men rise to greet me. Perr says, "Well met, Ilena. And what brings you back to us so soon?"

I look to Durant, who stands beside the chief. The swelling on his forehead is gone, and a smile lights his face. I feel a tremor that surprises me when our eyes meet. I force myself to turn to Perr. "Well met, sir. There is trouble at Dun Alyn, and Belert asks assistance from you"—I turn back to Durant—"and from Arthur's people."

"As we feared." The speaker is a short, gray-haired man who wears a single woolen garment draped around his body and shoulders in the old style. Tattoos much like Cochan's decorate his bare arms, but his face shows no marks of the painted ones.

Perr turns to the table and introduces me. "The lady Ilena came to us from the West. She is kin to those at Dun Alyn."

Spusscio speaks from behind me. "And through that kinship is heir to Dun Alyn."

The room is quiet. Durant watches me with an expression I can't read.

Perr breaks the silence. "You all know Spusscio, liege to Belert."

"And friend of Arthur's cause." A tall man with auburn hair and a flushed complexion stands and steps past me to greet Spusscio with a warrior's handclasp.

"This is Hoel, cousin to Arthur," Perr says to me. He turns back to the table and nods toward the gray-haired man. "Doldalf of Dun Selig." He indicates the woman seated at the end of the table. "Lenora of Glein."

Both stand and greet me. Lenora wears a woolen dress of deep red with a girdle worked in green leaves. Her long dark hair is unbound and held with a gold circlet. Despite the lady's costume, she has the broad shoulders and muscular arms of a warrior. Doldalf is dark, with the weathered look of a man who spends much time outdoors.

When all are seated again, and space on the benches has been found for me and Spusscio, Perr calls a servant girl. Soon Spusscio and I have ale and trenchers that hint of warm food to come.

Durant looks to me. "Will you tell us what brings you here?"

I look around the table and then to Spusscio with a question on my face.

Perr understands my concern. He says, "You can trust everyone here. All are pledged to Arthur's cause. Hoel and Durant are his emissaries here in the North. Lenora and Doldalf are chiefs of large holdings in this area. We meet now to consider the situation throughout the North and especially the rumors we've heard about Dun Alyn."

"If Lady Ilena permits, I will tell something of the matters at Dun Alyn," Spusscio says.

I try to keep relief out of my voice as I answer him. "Please, Spusscio. Go ahead."

As he begins, the servant returns with a kettle of meat and vegetables. I'm happy to eat while I listen.

"Ogern has been Druid of Dun Alyn since the time of his sister, Gwlech. When the first monks arrived, Gwlech and her children, Moren and Cara, accepted the new religion over Ogern's fierce objections.

"When Belert became Cara's husband, he supported her attempts to stop the sacrifices in the Oak

Grove and in time accepted the Christian faith himself. Ogern felt his own influence slipping away and became more and more determined to preserve the old ceremonies. He also plotted to keep Dun Alyn allied with the clans of the Far North.

"When Cara and Belert decided this past summer that Dun Alyn should join Arthur's alliance, Ogern increased his efforts. His friend, Resad, has been a frequent visitor to the fortress. Though Belert refused to believe it at first, I have good reason to think Ogern invited the attack that killed Miquain and Cara."

"And so we've come to believe," Hoel says. There is a general hum of agreement around the table.

Spusscio continues, "With Cara and Miquain gone, Ogern pushes his granddaughter as rightful heir to Dun Alyn. The child is daughter of Cara's cousin."

"And Ogern, of course, would be the real ruler," Lenora says.

Spusscio nods. "There was little way to counter that claim until Ilena arrived."

"And what is Ilena's claim?" Hoel asks.

Spusscio says, "Ilena is Moren's daughter."

"Ah," Perr says. "That is a valid claim."

Durant looks puzzled. "How so?"

Perr answers, "Moren was Cara's brother. Ilena then would be Cara's niece."

Durant nods. His expression is guarded when he looks at me.

Doldalf asks, "What assistance does Belert require of us?"

"Ogern has aroused people in the fortress," Spusscio says. "Ilena is so like Miquain in appearance that many believe she is Miquain herself, returned to us from the realm of the dead. As Samhain approaches, fears of such spirits heighten, and Ogern's power to weave spells in people's minds strengthens. As long as he can convince people that Ilena is a shapeshifter from the Sidth, they will not listen to anything Belert says. Your presence would bring order so Belert can advance Ilena's claim as heir."

Durant says, "You ask us then to ride and stand beside Belert as he declares Ilena chief of Dun Alyn."

Spusscio looks sideways at me. "The lady was sent to request that. I was given two instructions. One, to support her plea." He hesitates and looks at me again, then speaks slowly. "The second direction from Belert is that, should help not be available for us, I am, by whatever means necessary, to take the lady Ilena back safely to the Vale of Enfert."

I drop my dirk on the table and turn to him in shock. "I swore to fight for Dun Alyn. Do you and Belert take that promise lightly?"

"No. We know that you spoke sincerely and that you will keep your word. But Belert cannot bear to risk your life again."

"Again?" Durant's voice is sharp.

Spusscio says, "She was attacked at the fork on her way to Dun Alyn. When she was rescued by our war band and brought to the Great Hall, Ogern had her taken to a cage in the Oak Grove."

Doldalf asks me, "Who attacked you at the fork?"

"Those from beyond Red Mountain. And Resad was there," I answer.

"Resad!" Hoel says. "We hear much of Resad."

"Aye," Spusscio says. "He meets with the painted people from beyond Red Mountain and does Ogern's evil."

"Not just with those beyond Red Mountain, I'm afraid," Hoel says. "Saxons have sailed down into the Great Glen. They've made an alliance with those painted ones."

"Resad plays traitor not only to Dun Alyn but to all of Britain," Durant says. "Our sources name him as organizer of the alliance against Arthur in the North. It is likely that Ogern does Resad's bidding."

Lenora says, "So Dun Alyn could become a base on the coast for Saxons."

Hoel nods.

There is silence around the table. The servant refills our flagons, and Spusscio takes a chunk of meat on his dirk. I notice that I have eaten most of the food before me.

Perr breaks the silence. "Belert knows I will come to his aid."

Lenora asks, "What strength have we here?"

Perr says, "I can raise one hundred trained men and women with a day or two's notice during the spring and summer. Now, with winter approaching—"

Durant speaks. "I fear we don't have a day or two, Perr. Hoel has heard of a band from the Far North still below Red Mountain despite the season. And Ilena and I saw a small troop west of here several days ago. If we cannot wrest control of Dun Alyn from Resad and Ogern quickly, we may find it occupied by painted ones."

"And Saxons with them," Hoel adds. "I agree with the need for haste. I have three men with me."

"I brought a party of six," Lenora says.

Doldalf says, "Seven rode here with me."

"Twenty good warriors from Dreug to move at daybreak," Perr says.

"Some inside Dun Alyn will hold with Belert," Spusscio says.

"What say you, Ilena of Dun Alyn?" Durant asks. "Will that be enough?"

I count carefully. Forty-three and Belert with any who stand beside him. Moren once told me that fifty well-trained fighters were worth two hundred ordinary warriors. "It seems so to me. You are all wiser than I in warfare. What do you say?"

Perr says, "It is what we have, so it must be enough."

Doldalf nods in agreement. "It will be fine if we deal only with those at Dun Alyn. If others arrive we will do what we can."

Hoel and Durant exchange glances, and Durant speaks. "We will ride with you. I ask only one thing." He hesitates and looks at me. "The lady Ilena is important to this plan. She would be safer here at Dun Dreug. We can send for her when Dun Alyn is secure."

I am too surprised to speak. I look around the table. Hoel and Doldalf are nodding agreement. Lenora has an amused expression on her face. Spusscio watches me closely as does Perr. Finally I find my voice.

"I will not be left at Dun Dreug." I glare at Durant and turn to Spusscio. "I will not be taken to safety in the Vale of Enfert." I look around the table and measure out my words slowly, with as much emphasis as I can muster. "My place is at Dun Alyn. I ride out at daybreak."

Durant's lips tighten. He would like to say more, I know, but remains silent. The others make no argument. I sense that they approve of my stand.

Lenora speaks her thoughts. "Good! A chief does not seek safety while others fight her battles."

"Then let's get to bed," Perr says. "I'll send word to my people."

There is a general shuffling and scraping of benches. Spusscio nods to me and hurries out of the hall. I move slowly, hoping for a word with Durant.

He and Hoel are behind me. I can hear Hoel speaking. "Bad luck this, Durant. Your son will wait a few weeks longer to see his father."

"Aye," Durant says. "I promised him I'd try to return by Samhain. I hate to disappoint him."

I move on quickly, with no more desire for a private conversation. A son! My face burns with embarrassment. I did not think about a family. How foolish my thoughts have been. He said that he would be my brother, and I imagined he meant more. Of course he would be married. He is older than I, perhaps by ten years. How could I have let my feelings build with no evidence that they were appropriate?

I hurry into the women's quarters. The central hearth space is deserted, but the doorskins are pulled aside on three of the rooms. Gola is smoothing the bed in the room I used before; my pack is on the table beside a basin of steaming water.

"Thank you for waiting for me," I say. I long to talk to someone, to share my pain and disappointment, to confess my foolishness to someone who would understand. If Fiona were here, I would blurt out my feelings, but I haven't known Gola long enough yet to share such intimacies.

"I wanted to talk with you," she says. "And Cochan waits in the men's quarters for Spusscio. They are old friends."

"That water is welcome. I'm cold and dirty from traveling."

"I can bring more in the morning if you wish to bathe."

"Thank you, but I leave at first light."

Her face falls. "I was hoping to have a good visit with you. Must you return so soon?"

"Spusscio and I came for help. Chief Perr and the others will go back with us to aid Belert."

"If Perr plans to take a war band, Cochan and I will surely go along. At daybreak, you say?"

"Yes. I hope we can get there before nightfall the second day."

"If we leave early enough, and if snow holds off, we should manage that. I must prepare packs for Cochan and myself and be sure the kitchen can supply rations. May I leave you now?"

I puzzle over that question for a moment and then say, "Gola, I enjoy your company, but I can wash and dress myself. Go, and I will see you in the morning."

I drop the doorskin behind her and prepare for bed. The warm water feels good, but I don't linger over washing. It will be a short night. I try to think of the problems at Dun Alyn and what may be happening while Spusscio and I are gone, but I can't concentrate.

Durant's face when he bade me farewell last week and the smile when he saw me tonight seemed to send a message I wanted to hear. Hoel's words about a child told me something else. It doesn't make sense to me. There is only one thing I'm sure of. I must stop thinking about Durant.

I burrow into the bedskins, and my tired muscles relax. There is a pain in my heart that swells and pushes away sleep and sensible thought. At last I give in to it and weep. The pictures in my mind blur and blend until I do not know if I weep for Moren and Grenna, for Belert, or for myself.

CHAPTER 13

A HORN SOUNDS IN THE DARK. I HEAR VOICES AND THE jingle of harness. It seems the middle of the night, but I hear Lenora's voice outside my door. Another woman answers her, and their conversation fades as they move to the entrance. I pull the doorskin aside to let in light and warmth from the fire.

I dress as quickly as my tired body will move and carry my pack outside. The grounds are a jumble of horses and stable boys. Men and women in full battle dress move into the Great Hall. The sky is turning light with approaching dawn.

"Ilena. Over here." Gola's voice rises above the din. She motions for me to join her at the hall entrance. "Breakfast first. And gather enough food for your pack."

Inside, torches sputter around the walls, and the fire blazes. Durant sits with Hoel and Perr near the hearth.

He rises and comes to meet me. "Will you reconsider, Ilena? You would be safer here."

"No, Durant. I thought I spoke plainly last night." My voice is sharper than I intend.

He sighs. "Then will you remember that as a chief you must stay inside the fighting ring?"

I know that warriors try to protect their chiefs, but I also know that I must show leadership. I answer, "I will be careful. I hope that there is no battle, anyway. Belert believes the presence of his allies will stop opposition to me."

The horn sounds again, this time a series of quick notes in an urgent rhythm, and people begin to move out of the hall. I hurry to gather loaves and dried meat, and Gola brings me warmed ale.

"Drink this. You'll need it against the chill." She carries two waterskins. "I'll fill yours while you eat." She moves to a table that holds large pails of water.

Outside I find my gear on a tall roan mare. Rol, wearing a light halter, paces impatiently around a stable boy. Spusscio rides a small gray horse and leads his black mare. I am grateful to Perr's stablemaster. Our horses need more than one night's rest after such a strenuous trip. Rol doesn't appreciate the kindness and threatens to nip the roan when I mount her. I take his lead rein and pull his head up close beside me. There are other extra horses, most with packs, in the group.

I am amazed that such a large company could

gather on a few hours' notice. Durant and Hoel are near the gate. One of their companions raises a spear with Arthur's pennant on it. The bards often sing of the white dragon on a red background, but I've not seen it before. I feel a tremor of excitement as I watch it unfurl against the gray dawn sky.

Other pennants rise around the compound. Cochan holds one of blue with a gold boar, and a brown bear on green cloth snaps in the wind above Lenora's head.

Elban leaves Perr's side and rides over to me. "Chief Perr asks if you are ready, lady."

"Yes," I answer. Something more seems expected, but I don't know what.

He says, "Will you take the lead, then?"

I turn Rol and the roan toward the gate and hear the company move into place behind me. With Durant and Hoel on either side, the trumpet sounding its quick rhythm behind me, and the dragon pennant of Arthur streaming over my head, I ride through the gates of Dun Dreug out onto the track that leads to Dun Alyn.

The red rim of the rising sun greets us. It is a fair day for travel.

"Spusscio thinks we can reach Dun Alyn by late afternoon tomorrow. Do you agree?" Hoel asks.

I consider. "We have an early start, certainly. Days are short now that Samhain approaches, so it depends, I suppose, on how fast a group this size can travel." I remember our pace yesterday. "With Spusscio driving us on, we should certainly be there well before nightfall."

"Do you think we'll have trouble gaining entry to the fortress?"

"Spusscio will have a plan. And Belert will be watching for us." I hope that Belert is safe and able to watch for us and that he has found Ryamen. I steal a sideways glance at Durant. The sharp ache that kept me awake last night returns, and I look away quickly.

When we reach the turn where the trail leaves the streamside, I glance down the faint path that leads to Mona's Well. I wish there were time to stop and ask protection for our journey and for Belert's safety. Moren used to say that a warrior learned to pray on horseback. I can feel myself smiling as I think of him.

"You look cheerful, Ilena," Durant says. "When I saw you so grim this morning, I feared you were frightened. It would be natural, certainly, since we may have a battle on our hands."

"I am not frightened!" Surely it is only a small sin to lie at a time like this. Mock fighting with Moren was one thing. Actually being attacked or trying to kill someone else is quite another. I think back to the battle at the fork and feel the fear building inside me.

"You could let the rest of us go ahead and secure the fortress. That would be sensible."

I glare at him. "I am not frightened, and I will not stay behind!" I urge my horses forward until I am several yards ahead.

When we reach the first ascent, there is a short rest. Riders dismount and lead horses to a pool where water spurts out of the rock above. Standard-bearers stow pennants in their spear holders, and I watch Perr's trumpeter lash his instrument carefully on top of his pack.

After my horses have drunk their fill, I take their reins and head up the slope. My leg muscles ache at first, but the pain soon stops and I trudge on steadily. Spusscio is in the lead now, and Durant and Hoel are somewhere behind me.

When I reach the summit, the sun is directly overhead, lending welcome warmth to the day. I look below and see our party stretched far down the mountainside. A metallic jingle floats above the sounds of hooves and feet on the rocky track. Sunlight glints on helmets and sword hilts.

Hoel steps up beside me. "How far ahead is Spusscio?"

"I think he's just over the summit. He keeps stopping and waiting for us."

"I wish I had his energy," Hoel says.

I've thought the same thing several times on this trip. Hoel and I are both breathing heavily from the climb, and I hope Spusscio is ready to stop for a rest.

Durant and Perr join us. The horses stamp and blow while we stand quietly to watch the others approach.

Spusscio has come up behind us. "There's a spot

large enough for some of us a short distance down the other side. Let's push on." He speaks easily, as though he'd been strolling along a pleasant path instead of scrambling up a mountain.

I pull Rol and the mare into motion and follow him. Durant moves to walk beside me, but the trail narrows sharply, and he lets me go ahead. I'm glad. I am not ready to talk with him. I want to keep his friendship. A brother is a fine thing to have, but I cannot keep the pain out of my voice yet.

Spusscio's rest spot is a gentle slope just off the main trail. A stream splashes over a series of flat rock ledges. There isn't room for our entire group, but several horses at a time can water along the stream. I snatch a few minutes to sit before moving on to make room for those behind me.

Our night stop, hours later, is a strip of meadow that lies at the base of our next ascent. There is enough debris from shrubs and small trees to feed several fires. It is cold, and I am thankful we aren't higher. I roll myself in my own cloak and Ryamen's and fall asleep listening to quiet conversations around me.

I awaken to a whistling wind that moves down the valley. The only sounds close to me are the crackle from a dying fire and someone's snoring. The moon hangs just above the mountain across the valley, and clouds dim its light. I roll over and tighten my cloaks, but it is no use. I was too tired to find a place to relieve myself earlier, and now I cannot sleep.

I pull on my boots and move as quietly as possible among the sleeping forms to a jumble of large rocks just beyond the campsite.

As I come back around the rocks, I hear a shrill whine riding above the wind's whistle. Clouds are roiling fiercely now, and the moon casts a ghostly light that glimmers around them.

A footfall nearby startles me.

"Who . . . ?"

"Ilena?" Spusscio whispers from the other side of a boulder.

"Is it the Wild Hunt?" I ask.

"Aye." He pulls himself up onto the rock. "The Hounds of Gwynn. We always hear them this close to Samhain." He looks up into the sky, where a number of dark, V-shaped lines move from north to south.

I shiver and pull my cloak tighter. The noise strengthens, and the wind increases. "The monks call them the Gabriel Hounds," I say.

"Gwynn ran his hounds of the Wild Hunt long before the monks came."

The unearthly sounds are swelling around us. According to the old stories, Gwynn, huntsman of the otherworld, with hounds howling behind him, gathers the dead and takes them to the Sidth. Some say anyone outdoors is in danger when the hunt rides. Folk in Enfert huddle in their homes until the sounds pass by.

I think back to the first time that I associated the stories told in the village with the noise above our home. I seem for a moment to be there with Grenna, weaving by firelight, the shrieks outside drowning out the clack of the loom. The house was filled with the sharp smells of thyme and pennyroyal, remedies for the colds and fevers of winter, that Grenna and I had gathered that day. Large bundles lay drying on a bench by the fire.

Moren was bending over the table cutting a piece of leather for a harness strap when he heard them. I can see his head raised, his eyes alert, as he listened to the din.

Grenna noticed me cowering on my bedplace, looking, I suppose, as frightened as I felt. "Moren, look. The lass is terrified."

I haven't heard her voice for over two years, but the memory is so clear and true, she could be beside me now.

Moren scooped me up and carried me out into the crisp fall night. "It's all right, Ilena. Nothing has ever come down out of the sky."

We stood side by side and looked up. He pointed to the long, V-shaped lines moving across the moon's face. "What the storytellers don't say is that wild geese are always overhead when we hear the sound. Call them what you like, the Hounds of Gwynn or the Gabriel Hounds, but know that they are really geese going south for the winter, and they'll return in the spring."

Grenna joined us and put her arm around my

shoulder. "Aye, lass, though it's a time to remember the ones we've lost, sure enough."

"Yes," Moren said. "But no need to fear the Gabriel Hounds. They wish us no harm."

Spusscio is saying something. I become aware of the hard boulder against my shoulders and the cold wind whipping my hair. "I'm sorry, Spusscio. I didn't hear you."

"You seemed far away. I was talking of Cara and Miquain."

"Aye, we all have loved ones to mourn this Samhain," I say.

He is silent for a time. The honking streams of geese pass on to the south, and the wind quiets. He jumps down from the boulder and turns to me. "Tomorrow will be a hard day, lady. Try to sleep."

I reach out and take his hand in a warrior's clasp. "I am glad I stumbled over you at Dun Alyn."

A wide cloud has passed over the moon, and I cannot see his face. I sense a smile, though, as he replies, "A good meeting for me too, lady, and for Dun Alyn."

I pick my way back to my sleeping place by the dim glow from low fires. The wind has calmed, and the geese are gone. I go to sleep easily and waken almost immediately, it seems, to the trumpet calling us to the day's march.

We prepare in darkness and move up the second slope as dawn is breaking. Rol is frisky and climbs readily behind me. I have harnessed and saddled him.

One of Perr's men has the roan now; his own mount went lame in the boulder field yesterday. We reach the overlook on the east side of the mountain well before noon.

On the outcrop Durant, Perr, Spusscio, and I scan the landscape before us. The sea in the distance is a bright blue, and the sky holds no sign of clouds.

Durant says, "The weather has held for us. I hope it lasts a few more days."

He is thinking of his family, I suppose. Well, I will not keep him at Dun Alyn.

Spusscio has been staring at one spot to the north for some time. He raises his arm and points a short finger. There are hills past the wildwood and well beyond the fork in the trail. They look to lie a good distance northwest of Dun Alyn.

"By the gods!" Durant mutters.

"Several of them," Perr adds.

I strain to see what they are watching. The hills roll dark and tree-covered to the horizon. There are lines that mark breaks in the trees for tracks or streams. A ray of light gleams along one of the lines. Then another. Finally I understand.

The sun glints off of something shiny in several places along one of the treeless strips. Helmets, armor, weapons, shields, harness fittings are shiny. A war band on the march would look like that. The distance between some of the reflections suggests a large group.

"Could it be a hunting party?" I ask.

"Too big," Spusscio grunts.

"Is there another fortress anywhere in that area?" Durant asks.

"No." Perr and Spusscio speak in unison.

Doldalf and Lenora have joined us and watch glumly.

Hoel climbs up with us and gazes north. "The painted ones we've heard about?"

Durant answers, "Probably, and a few Saxons in the bunch, I'd guess. We don't know of another war band that size anywhere in the area."

"Then it's a race for Dun Alyn." Spusscio turns to go back to his horse.

"Will they have to go through the fork?" Perr asks.

Spusscio stops to consider. "There is an old track that joins the road to the fortress just below the gate. They might know it."

"If Resad is directing them, they would have any information about the defenses they need," Durant says.

"Aye," Spusscio says, "and we must get to the gates before they enter and barricade them."

He too has returned his borrowed horse and saddled his own. Now he throws the lead rein over the saddle pommel, leaving the mare free to find her own way, and plunges ahead down the rocky descent.

I follow his example and make as good time as I can with Rol close behind. When the two of us reach the bottom, we turn to look back. Our horses are picking their way toward us a short distance up the trail. Durant, Perr, and the others are far behind them.

The black mare reaches the valley floor ahead of Rol, and Spusscio is mounted and gone before I have caught my breath. When Rol trots up to me, I leap onto his back and set him after Spusscio at a hard gallop.

We stop to rest the horses at the edge of the wildwood and let them drink.

Spusscio says, "It would be best if you waited for the others, lady."

"Best for whom, Spusscio?" I ask. "Belert is in danger, especially now that Ogern has support to take over Dun Alyn."

"I know," he says. "That is why I hurry. Even a dwarf can be of some help."

"Well then, a woman and a dwarf should be of more help than a dwarf alone."

He smiles and says no more.

The troops behind us are starting across the valley now. We splash across the river and enter the forest with the horses at a steady gallop. When we approach the fork, Spusscio pulls the mare up, and I stop Rol beside him. We listen for a time but hear nothing.

"They're for the old trail, then," he says. "Resad would have told them." He heads the mare down the track toward Dun Alyn.

When we move out onto the road that leads up to the fortress, I see a party of five riders moving through the first entrance. I cannot tell who they are, but one has a large black horse.

Spusscio points to a spot north and west of the fortress where a trail comes out of the woods. A war band is moving toward Dun Alyn.

Spusscio gathers his shield and loosens a war spear from its holder. "Will you go back to meet the others?"

"What are you going to do?" I ask.

"I can get to the gate before they reach this road. I want to be at Belert's side. Durant and Perr must know what the situation is so they can be prepared."

I am eager to be with Belert too, but I understand what Spusscio means. I say, "Godspeed, then. I will join you inside as soon as I can." I turn Rol around and hurry back to our troop.

Perr's banner flies at the front of the band, with Arthur's just behind. I stop Rol a short distance ahead of them and turn him so that I fall in alongside Durant and Perr. When I describe the scene at Dun Alyn, both men urge their horses to a faster gait.

"Do we want the horns?" Perr asks.

"Not yet," I say. "The painted ones are well armed, but they move without urgency. They have no reason to expect an attack outside the fortress. If we can get close before they know we're here, we may be able to hold them outside."

Durant nods and turns to the ones behind. "Pass the word to hurry, but no horns or calls until they see us." He turns back and puts Bork to a hard gallop.

Rol keeps pace and we break out into the open meadow below the fortress before the rest. We raise shields and pull our spears from their fittings as we ride. I cannot see Spusscio and assume he is inside the fortress.

Ten of the painted ones have turned onto the road that leads up to Dun Alyn, while the rest are spread out along the narrow track from the woods. When they hear us, the ten ahead stop and turn to block the way.

Horns sound and shouts begin from the enemy and then from our force. I raise the call Moren taught me, the battle cry of Dun Alyn, and set Rol straight for the warriors across the path ahead. Durant is on one side of me, and Hoel is on the other. I hear a woman's voice—Lenora's, I think—in a bloodcurdling series of notes and syllables behind me.

The ones across the path seem stunned at first. Before they can raise shields and aim spears, we are upon them. My spear takes a tall, heavily tattooed man at the waist. His leather vest holds against the iron, but the force topples him off his horse. Rol's charge carries us through their lines and out onto the road behind them. I slow him, and we wheel around to face the battle.

I pause to determine the most important point to charge. The ten who blocked the road are losing ground under fierce attack. Three are in the dust, and as I watch, Durant unhorses another. Lenora wields her sword in a whirling arc that endangers anyone within striking distance.

Most of our people have turned onto the narrow track to engage the attackers before they reach the road. I see Cochan with Perr's banner over his head and Gola beside him. The war band of Northmen is being beaten back onto their own ranks. Supply horses are slowing the movement to the rear and causing a jumble of warriors and animals throughout the troop.

I turn Rol again and head to the first entrance of Dun Alyn. The sentries put lances across the opening when they see me coming. As I draw nearer, they lower the weapons and leap back.

"It is the lady Miquain!"

"She returns when we need her."

Both stare at me open-mouthed as I guide Rol through the entry. We are moving now at a quick walk. A faster speed and Rol would not be able to make the turns into the ring and through the second entrance.

There the response is the same. The sentries seem to fear me, but no one challenges me.

At the inner entrance to the compound, I recognize the young men who laughed at Spusscio when we left four days ago. The gate is open, but they race to close it against me. I speak to Rol, and he lunges toward them with such force that they let go of the gate and leap out of the way. We pass through with a light scrape of my boot against the logs.

CHAPTER 14

THE FORTRESS GROUNDS ARE ALMOST DESERTED. A woman drags her child into a house while another races to a stable, calling out for her son. Most people seem to have taken refuge already from whatever is to come.

I can hear Ogern's voice above a noise of horses and weapons from the side of the main stable. I move closer and turn Rol in against a wall where we won't be seen. Ogern's voice rises and falls in hypnotic cadences.

"The ones from the North are our allies. They ride here now to assist us against Arthur's men."

A voice calls out, "And where is our chief? I am sworn to stand beside Belert."

Ogern answers, "Belert is mad. He can no longer lead you. His decisions are flawed."

"Where is he?" another voice asks.

"I do not know," Ogern says. "If he were able to

lead you, would he not be here when a battle rages outside our gates?"

There is a confusion of voices. One sounds above the others. "Then let us hold from the battle. It is not clear to me that we should ally with the painted ones."

"Aye. Until we have a council we cannot determine the wisest course."

Ogern's voice is shrill. "I tell you we must drive Arthur's men from our gates. They would drag us into alliance with old enemies in the South."

"I don't care what you say, Ogern. I'm for pushing the painted ones back behind Red Mountain where they belong. If Arthur's men oppose them, I fight under the dragon."

I pull Rol back farther into a space between two houses as a group of horsemen leaves the stable area and heads for the gate. As they pass through the entrance, I can see a banner with black background and a goshawk outlined in white needlework. The familiar battle cry begins as they move out of sight into the inner ring.

Ogern's voice still sounds from the other side of the building. "Let them go, then. The rest of you follow me! We'll force Arthur's men out of the North and ally with Northmen."

The voice I heard first speaks again. "I'll wait here, Ogern. I've no desire to get into a fight when I'm not sure which side I'm on. I still want to hear from

Belert. He's our chief, and we have no reason to abandon him."

"He won't be chief for long. Cara is dead. Remember?" Ogern's voice is hoarse from shouting.

"I'll wait here, too. If the fight comes inside, I'll decide who to join." This is a new voice. Ogern is having little success.

The group around Ogern seems to be staying there, so I ease Rol out from between the houses and head him down the center courtyard toward the Great Hall. As I approach, I can see the reason Belert is not at the head of his war band.

The five horsemen who entered the gates ahead of Spusscio are behind the Great Hall. Spusscio is there also; his black mare rears and plunges as he attempts to keep the five away from his chief. Belert, sword drawn, stands beside Cormec. Resad must have brought the others straight back to Belert's quarters.

When I reach the group, I signal Rol. He rears and strikes at a big gray stallion. Spusscio uses the distraction to unhorse a man whose face is covered with blue tattoos. Cormec leaps forward and pulls another from his horse. I find myself face to face with Resad. My shield takes the blow from his sword, and I attempt to thrust behind his guard. He is too quick for me; my sword glances off his shield. The interchange moves us past each other, and I turn Rol to join Spusscio in maintaining a defense between the attackers and Belert. Cormec has dispatched the man he pulled to the ground and moved back beside Belert. Resad and his two companions still on horseback push against us, and Resad's black stallion attacks Rol. Staying in the saddle takes all my attention for a time.

With our horses rearing and plunging, Resad and I try to keep shields in place and exchange sword thrusts. Our activity takes us past the living quarters and back near the rampart wall. I pull Rol's head down and force him to move away from the other horse. I need to regain control of him and try to move in on Resad's left side. I shift my shield to my right arm and my sword to my left before I urge Rol back to charge my opponent again.

The ruse works, and we are upon him before he realizes what I have done. Even if he can handle a sword with his left hand, he does not have time to shift before I attack. He keeps his shield in place but cannot reach across effectively with his sword. I keep thrusting and finally unhorse him with a strong blow that glances off his shield and onto his helmet.

He rolls over in the dust and tries to regain his feet. I dismount and move in to disarm him before he can stand. Out of the corner of my eye I see Rol advance against the black horse. I kick Resad's sword arm as he is clambering to his feet. He loses his balance and sprawls on the ground. His sword flies out of his hand. I wait, holding my sword, until he rolls over.

When his eyes meet mine, there is no fear, no sign

that he's at my mercy. Instead, I see the same mocking smile I remember from our encounter at the fork.

Suddenly an arm locks around my neck, and I am jerked backward. I try to swing my sword over my head but stop when I feel the sharp edge of a dirk against my throat.

Resad scrambles to his feet and takes my sword and shield from me. He lays them in the dirt and picks up his own blade. "Looks like we have her."

"Yes." It is Ogern's voice in my ear. "We'll be sure she's dealt with this time."

"We dare not kill her here," Resad says.

"Out the back exit. We'll throw her in the pit with the other one. We can dispose of her later."

My battle with Resad has carried us far from Belert and Spusscio. I can see Rol in the distance still fighting with Resad's stallion, but no one is in a position to notice that I need help. When I open my mouth to call out, Ogern tightens the blade against my throat.

They drag me along beside the rampart wall toward the back entrance. I can hear battle sounds in the distance and, closer, the noise of fighting stallions; otherwise the fortress is quiet. If Belert and Spusscio still engage Resad's allies, the sounds are too muffled to hear at this distance.

We reach a wide ladder that leads to the top of the rampart wall. The back entrance is ahead of us, and I can hear surf roaring below the wall beside us.

"Ilena! Ilena!" It is Durant's voice. "Ilena! Where are

you?" He sounds close for a moment, then farther as he moves on toward the Great Hall.

I struggle to speak, and the dirk cuts into my skin. I freeze in place and feel warm blood trickle down my neck. Resad steps to my side and grasps my arm. The shouts grow close again. Now I can hear Belert's voice. Both men call my name. I want to answer, but I know the knife will finish its job if I try.

"Hold, Ogern!" Belert's voice rings with authority. He appears from between two houses with his sword raised. When he sees the dirk at my throat, he lowers his weapon and stops.

Resad lets go of my arm and steps in front of Ogern and me.

"Let her go." Durant has come up beside Belert. "Your forces are retreating outside the walls. You'll not gain anything by harming her."

Resad speaks to Ogern. "Get her up on the ramparts! I'll keep them here."

Ogern pulls me to the ladder and begins climbing. At first I move as slowly as I can, but the dirk presses harder, and I climb with him. There are shouts and sounds of a scuffle below. Ogern pauses, then moves faster. He is gulping deep, ragged breaths now, and I can feel his heart racing against my back. I hear the clash of sword on sword behind us.

We climb onto the walltop, and I catch a glimpse of the fight at the bottom of the ladder. Resad and Durant are trading sword thrusts. Belert is trying to edge past them to get onto the steps.

Ogern drags me along the rampart to a section that lies directly above the cliff. A wicker wall rises shoulder-high around most of the fortress. Here on the sea side there is no danger from slingstones or arrows, so there is no shield. The stone outer shell of the rampart rises less than knee-high above the earthen walkway. When we stop, the view is straight down onto surf-drenched rocks far below.

I am terrified as I guess Ogern's intentions.

"Ogern!" Belert's voice sounds behind us.

Ogern whirls us around.

Belert stands, sword in hand, a few feet from us. "Let her go. The lass has never harmed you."

"Never harmed me? She keeps me from my rightful place as ruler of Dun Alyn. I should have been chief when my sister died, but Cara brought you here. You encouraged her to leave the old ways. Now I will be chief, and Dun Alyn will return to the ancient truths."

"You have been Druid since long before I came," Belert says. "You have been a good Druid, with your people's welfare always your first concern."

"It is still my concern," Ogern says. "You supported Cara in forcing me to stop the rituals in the Oak Grove. When you deserted the old religion, Dun Alyn fell farther and farther from its true path."

"We have not deserted the old ways," Belert says.

"Cara ordered you to stop the human sacrifices. That is the only change."

"No. You ally us with enemies from the West and the South and even try to make a pact with Arthur. His people have never been our friends."

I can feel Ogern's breathing get faster and faster. Belert is inching toward us. It takes a few moments for Ogern to notice.

"Stop! Don't come any closer." I feel his arm tighten around my waist. The knife quivers against my throat.

Belert is motionless now. "Let her go, Ogern. You already have the deaths of Cara and Miquain on your head. Do not kill another innocent woman."

Ogern's voice is shrill now and he speaks rapidly. "I warned them. 'Stay inside,' I said. I would have made peace with the attackers. Resad speaks their language. But they raced out to do battle." He backs closer to the low outside wall that edges the rampart and swings me around so that I am next to the drop-off.

Belert lays his sword on the walkway. His voice is quiet but his words are clear. "Let Ilena go. I will take her place. When you've killed me, she will go away and leave you in control."

I can feel Ogern's body tense as he considers this.

"If you hurt her, I will not let you live. If you release her, I will stand before you unarmed." The chief takes the dirk from his belt and drops it beside the sword. He moves a step closer to us.

I watch his face. He is sincere. He will put himself in my place.

The Druid yells, "Do not step closer. This one must die. I will deal with you when I am chief."

"If Ilena is harmed, before God and myself, you will not survive to leave this rampart." Belert moves another step.

Ogern shifts closer to the edge. My leg presses against the low stone bulwark, and I can see rocks and surf below. We sway together, and Belert pales. Ogern steps backward again and stumbles. The pressure on my throat eases. The knife clatters onto the walkway. I jerk my head back hard against my captor's shoulder and twist against the arm that binds me to him. The motion throws him farther off balance, and he loses his grip around my waist.

I try to lunge forward, away from him, but he grasps at my arm and hangs on to me. I jerk and twist to free myself. He falls, screaming, over the side and drags me with him.

I catch the top of the wall with my free arm and hang on. Ogern dangles for a terrifying moment from my other arm but loses his grip and crashes onto the rocks far below.

I seem to hang there for a long time. My right arm aches with the weight of my body.

Belert's voice sounds above the surf and wind. "Grab my hand. It's to your left—up. Up a little more."

I scrape my left forearm over the rough wall until I

find his hand. I grasp it and feel some of the pressure leave my right shoulder. He pulls until I can grasp the top of the wall with my left hand too. I hang like that for a few moments, with both hands clamped onto the walltop and Belert clasping my wrists.

"I'm going to let go of one arm," he yells. "Hang on, and I'll try to reach farther so I can pull you up."

There is a sickening jolt in my stomach as I feel his hand release my left wrist. I force myself to keep from screaming and try to push my body closer to the wall.

He grasps my left upper arm and says, "Now I'll let go of your right wrist."

When he has my right arm secure, we both rest. I can hear his hoarse breathing just above my head.

"If you're ready," he says, "we'll do this again so I can get a better hold."

This time I end up higher on the wall with his hands under my armpits. I can hook my forearms over the top of the wall. He begins to tug me upward. I try to brace my feet against the wall and walk my way up, but the stone is too wet from sea mist to give any traction for my boots.

Suddenly I feel a pair of strong hands clamp around my waist, and I swing up over the wall. Durant is trembling as he stands me down safely on the rampart floor.

The three of us, Belert still kneeling with his arms resting on the walltop, and Durant and I supporting each other where we stand, look at one another in silence.

There are footsteps on the ladder, and we turn to watch Spusscio appear. His relief at finding us shows on his face.

Belert struggles to his feet and rests his hand on my shoulder.

Spusscio says, "I've been searching." He turns back to the stairs and calls, "Cormec! They're up here. Safe. Both of them. And Durant."

When none of us speaks, he continues. "I saw Resad's body." He nods to Durant. "You?"

"Aye," Durant says. "A hard fighter, that one."

"And Ogern?" Spusscio asks.

Belert points over the rampart.

Spusscio walks to the edge and looks down. He stares at Ogern's body sprawled below with an expression I can't read, then turns to me. "Are you all right, lady?"

I nod. "Thanks to Belert . . . and Durant."

"How goes it outside?" Belert asks.

"Well enough," Durant answers. "A troop from Dun Alyn joined us, and the Saxons and painted ones retreated quickly. They make camp now on the edge of the woods to tend their wounded. I'd guess they'll be gone in the morning."

Cormec's voice comes from the ladder. "I've brought a torch. Are you coming down?"

The sun has set; we stand in near-darkness on the rampart. The sea wind has freshened, and I shiver with cold. Durant pulls me close to him. His hand feels warm on my cold arm. I let myself lean against him for a moment before I recall Hoel's words. I stiffen then and move away. He drops his hand and steps back.

I try to pretend I've recovered from my fright, but my wobbly legs betray me. Belert notices and offers his arm to steady me as I clamber down the ladder. Once on the ground I take deep breaths and force my body to behave. I cannot see Resad's body in the pool of light from the torch, but I don't look too carefully around us.

Cormec holds the torch beside the steps until Spusscio and Durant are down, then turns to Belert. "Your troops are asking about you, sir. Will you speak with them?"

"Aye," Belert replies. "How many stayed with us?"

"About twenty-five rode out to join the fight. The rest refused to follow Ogern and waited inside to see what would happen."

Belert nods and turns to me. "Will you join me, Ilena? All know by now that you brought the forces from Dreug and from Arthur."

"Dun Selig and Glein are here also," I say.

"Did Lenora and Doldalf ride with you?" He sounds pleased.

We've come out of a narrow passage between houses into the central courtyard. It is a noisy jumble of horses, dogs, and people now. Torches blaze around the grounds, and large bonfires are flaring in several places. I can see the white goshawk of Dun Alyn still flying from its spear point near the front gate. A group of warriors stands around it. Arthur's dragon snaps in the wind near the stable.

Durant says, "I'll leave you now; I need to check on my companions." He heads toward the dragon pennant.

"And I'll be wanted in the surgery." Spusscio hurries off to a long building across the compound.

"We'll talk with our people first, then go round to the others," Belert says. When I drop behind him, he stops and takes my arm to keep me beside him.

Cormec walks on my other side with the torch high enough to keep smoke and ashes out of our faces. When we reach the group by the gate, he speaks first. "I've found Belert for you. He was on the rampart tending to the traitors who brought the enemy against us."

A stocky, bearded man in the forefront of the troop speaks. "Aye. Two of the sentries were part of Ogern's plot. They've been dealt with."

Belert says, "The lady Ilena dispatched Ogern, and Durant from Arthur's table defeated Resad. Cormec was with me, as he has been these past two days. My thanks to all of you for defending Dun Alyn."

"We are glad to see you well," the man says, "and the lady."

I'm not sure whether the last is a question or not, but Belert takes it as one.

He says, "The lady Ilena is Cara's nearest kin. I will meet with the elders tomorrow to speak of her claim as heir to Dun Alyn. And now, if there are no more questions, we must greet those who rode to our aid."

The group breaks up, talking among themselves. Those with horses head for the stables. I wonder about Rol; I am eager to look for him.

We meet with each group that rode to Dun Alyn with me. Belert inquires about injuries, points out the guest sleeping quarters, and assures everyone that cooks are laying out food and ale in the Great Hall.

In the surgery we find Doldalf with fresh bandages on a shoulder wound. He reaches up from the bedplace with his good arm to clasp Belert's hand. "We ran them off proper for you."

"Aye," Belert says, "and you know you have my thanks."

"Sure, and you'll do the same for me, I know—and have, as I remember."

"What's that?" Belert points to the bandages.

"One of the painted ones actually aimed his spear. It's of no matter."

Spusscio has come up to us. "Another bit deeper and it would matter, Doldalf. And don't forget you're to lie here without moving until the bleeding stops."

"What a tyrant you are, Spusscio," Doldalf says. "It

had better be fixed in another day. I ride back home, bleeding or not."

Spusscio shakes his head. "Thank your gods you're as tough as an ox, old man. It'll probably be all right. There's enough spiderwebs bound on it and a good egg white besides."

"It's the waste of the ale cleaning it that I mind." Doldalf manages a laugh.

"I'll bring you ale to drink," Belert says, "and supper if you're ready for it."

"Aye," Doldalf says. "I can eat, I'm sure."

I put my hand on his good arm. "I thank you for riding with me. I'll look in tomorrow to see how the shoulder is."

Two of Lenora's people are in the surgery. A woman lies with a poultice bandaged over a swelling on her cheek.

"A slingstone?" I ask.

"Yes, lady. Thank the gods it glanced off. I'll stay down tonight to let it heal."

The other, a young man near my age, is sleeping. His leg is bandaged and splinted. Ropes are fixed to keep it in one place.

"The potions haven't worn off yet," Spusscio says. "The surgeon had to work to get that leg set, and we dosed him pretty heavily."

"What happened?" I ask.

"Lenora told us his horse went down. It rolled over

on him and snapped the leg." Spusscio checks one of the ropes and eyes a bloodstain on the bandage. "I hope it's stopped bleeding. He'll stay here with us for a while, I reckon."

"Will you be coming to the Great Hall soon for some supper?" Belert asks.

"Aye," Spusscio says. "As soon as I'm sure everything here is in place."

"We'll go on, then," Belert says. He heads for the door.

I hurry to catch up. "I'll stop by the stables first. I want to find out what happened to Rol."

He says, "You must be exhausted by now. Don't wait too long to get food and some sleep."

I assure him that I plan to do both soon and head for the barns.

I find Rol in the stable unharnessed and rubbed down. The stablemaster is working on Resad's big black three stalls away.

"Where did you find them?" I ask.

"They'd worn themselves out fighting," he says. "This one has a nasty bite. Yours looks all right."

I talk to Rol to calm him. I can't see any injuries, and the stablemaster has done a fine job of drying him off and giving him a little water. I say, "Thank you for taking care of him."

The man nods. Then he asks, "What about Resad?"

"He'll not need his horse again."

The man looks at me for a moment, but says only, "Your pack is there beside the stall door, lady."

People are coming and going at the Great Hall. Several of our troops sit at a table near the hearth, with Perr, Hoel, and Durant together at one end. Lenora is filling an ale flagon at a cauldron near the hearth. Gola sees me before I can pick her out of the group.

"Ilena!" She hurries to my side. "Are you well? We lost sight of you when the fighting started. Where did you go?"

"I came inside to be sure Belert was guarded," I say. As we walk by the fire, she grabs my arm and turns me toward the blaze.

"What happened to your neck?" She lifts my chin and studies the wound left by Ogern's dirk.

"What is it?" Durant asks. He has left the table and joins Gola in peering at my throat.

"A scratch."

"A dirk cut, it looks like," Durant says. "When did he do that?"

I decide not to tell him that it was when I heard his voice. "I tried to call for help," I say.

He traces the wound with a gentle finger. I brace myself against my feelings, but it is no use. I feel the soft ache inside and turn away quickly. He drops his hand and goes back to the table.

"It's shallow," Gola says. "Who did it?"

I answer her questions while I slice a trencher and

pile meat on it. Gola fills a flagon with ale for me. We join the others. Their talk is of the return trip.

Cochan says, "We'll stay, certainly, for the feast tomorrow."

"Aye," Perr says, "but no longer. The snow cannot hold off forever."

Durant says, "We want to see Ilena safely established as chief of Dun Alyn."

"There should be no problem with that," Hoel says. "Ogern and Resad were the obstacles. I haven't found anyone in the fortress who opposes her now."

"With Belert in charge again, that's no surprise," Lenora says. "Most will forget they were ready to turn against him."

"It is hard for folk," Perr says. "Their family's lives and their own depend on keeping favor with the strongest contender in a dispute like this."

"But some stay loyal." I think of Cormec and Spusscio.

"Yes, thank the gods," Lenora says.

As we talk, men and women from Dun Alyn come and go in the hall. Many sit down to eat and drink. Some carry food and ale out with them. All gaze at me curiously from time to time, but I see little sign of the fear that my presence brought at first. Belert's news about me must have spread.

I cannot keep from yawning. My body hurts all over. I stand to go but remember my new role. "Are you all in quarters?"

"Aye," Gola says. "Spusscio saw to it." She stands and reaches for my hand. "A good sleep, now."

"And a good rest for you." I nod to include all at the table.

I find Miquain's room open and a night fire at the hearth. A young woman I've not seen before is pulling back bedskins.

"My lady." She seems shy but not especially fearful. "Spusscio sent me to serve you. I was the lady Miquain's maidservant." There are tears in her eyes when she speaks of Miquain, and she turns to hide them.

"Thank you," I say. I lay my pack on the table and sit on the bench to pull off my boots. She hurries to help me.

The bed is as comfortable as I remember, and I barely mumble my goodnight as she leaves. My last thoughts are of Belert's face when Ogern pushed me to the side of the rampart.

CHAPTER 15

I AWAKEN EARLY FROM A DREAM OF RYAMEN. SHE CALLED to me, but I could not find her. There was something important about it, but I can't remember what it was. I dress and go out onto the grounds.

The tall gates are open, and a hunting party moves through them with a pack of hounds milling around the horses' legs. One dog, speckled and frisky, reminds me of Cryner when he was young. He used to prance around our horses like that when we went out to hunt.

I walk to the entrance and look across the meadow where the track winds out of the woods. There is no sign of anyone camped there. The war band must have moved on at the first hint of daylight.

Cooking smells waft across the compound from the kitchen area. A whole beef is turning above a bed of glowing coals, and nearby a kitchen boy kneels to fan a blaze inside a rock-filled firepit. Perhaps the hunt this morning is for the boar that will roast there the rest of the day.

I watch the boy as he kneels and reaches down. There is something familiar about the scene. I was kneeling so in my dream. Ryamen was down in a hole or well of some sort. Then I remember Ogern's words "... the back exit... in the pit with the other one." I see Spusscio leaving the stables and run toward him.

"Spusscio! Spusscio! Ryamen—I remember!"

We meet in the center of the compound.

I gasp in my haste to explain. "Ogern. Last night. He told Resad to put me in the pit with the other one. He must have meant Ryamen."

Spusscio turns back to the stables, and I follow him.

"Cormec!" his voice echoes through the first barn. "Cormec, where are you?"

"Here, Spusscio." Cormec appears from a stall near the far end. "What now? You have too much energy for such an early hour."

"The old pits," Spusscio says. "You remember them?"

"Of course," Cormec answers. "I don't want to know what the old ones used them for. Some grisly bones down in those things."

"Ogern planned to put Ilena in a pit with the 'other one.' "

Cormec thinks for a minute. "Ryamen! Why didn't we think of looking there?"

"Get horses. And rope." Spusscio turns to me. "Bring food and water. I'll fetch a chariot."

When I return from the kitchen with a loaf of bread and a waterskin, Spusscio is placing a coil of rope on the saddle pommel of a brown mare. A gray mare is saddled for me, and Cormec is fastening the last straps on a pair of blacks harnessed to a wicker chariot.

We leave by the front gates and circle around the fortress to head north. Spusscio and I are soon far ahead of Cormec. He is slowed by the task of maneuvering the chariot through the defensive rings and over uneven ground.

The pits lie north of Dun Alyn, along the cliffs above the sea. The first two we examine are empty except for bones and evidence in one of a long-ago fire. They are deeper than the ones I've seen for storing grain. A man standing on another's shoulders could not reach the top of one of these.

I cannot see any other pits around us. "Are there more?" I ask.

"Aye," Spusscio says. "One more."

We ride on to a desolate space beside a cave entrance. We tie the horses, and Spusscio, the coil of rope on his shoulder, leads the way through a rim of boulders into a small hollow. There amid scrubby bushes and coarse grass is another pit. It is as deep as the others, but it is not empty.

What looks at first like a pile of cloth is crumpled

against one side of the circular clay floor in a pool of morning sunlight.

"Ryamen," Spusscio calls. "Can you hear me?"

There is no response. She lies motionless. I cannot tell if she is breathing. In the distance I can hear chariot wheels grating against the rocky trail.

"Will you bring the water, lady? I hope we'll have use for it." As he talks, he wraps the rope around a large boulder and ties it securely.

When I return with the waterskin and bread, he is out of sight, and the rope is taut with his weight. I watch anxiously as he drops onto the pit bottom and hurries to Ryamen. Her body is limp when he lifts her head, but I can see her eyelids flutter and her lips move. I drop the container carefully, and he moistens her lips with water. She moves her head slightly, and Spusscio tips the waterskin again. I can see her throat move as she swallows.

"Is she alive?" Cormec comes up behind me.

"Yes, but not fully conscious," I answer. "How can we get her out?"

"These weren't made to get anyone out of," he says. "But I brought a hide and another rope. We'll manage."

I would like to go down to see how Ryamen is for myself, but I settle for watching Spusscio work. Cormec drops a bundle that proves to be a large, tanned ox hide. He follows it with another coil of rope. Spusscio spreads the skin out and lifts Ryamen into the center. He wraps her in the hide and loops rope several times around the unwieldy bundle. He ties off the rope and knots the end of line that dangles down from the top through the loops around the hide.

When Spusscio is finished, Cormec begins to pull on the line. Ryamen, in her ox-hide case, rises slowly upward. Spusscio steadies her away from the sides of the pit for as long as he can reach her. I drop flat on my belly and stretch to reach first the rope and then the bundle itself to keep it from banging against the wall. When she reaches the top, I grasp the hide and pull her onto level ground.

I fold the skin back and brush dirt from her face. She is still, and her eyes are closed, but I can see the gentle movement as she breathes.

Cormec unties the rope and drops the end down to Spusscio. With a few tugs and a scrambling noise, he is beside us. He takes the waterskin off his shoulder and hands it to me. I pour a little water onto a piece of soft bread from the inside of the loaf. When I hold it against Ryamen's mouth, she turns her head slightly to refuse it.

"Let's get her to the chariot," Spusscio says. "She needs broth and a warm bed."

We place her, still wrapped in the ox hide, on the floor of the chariot. I brace myself across the open back and hold her head in my lap. Cormec ties my horse's rein to the chariot rim and steps over me to get in the driver's position.

Spusscio rides ahead. Cormec holds the horses to a

slow walk until we reach a smooth surface, then speeds them toward the entrance to the fortress.

At Ryamen's house Spusscio has a fire blazing and the bedplace ready. The woman working with mortar and pestle at the table is stooped with age. She turns her head to one side and squints up at us as we enter. When she focuses on Cormec with the bundle, she hurries to help us. We lay Ryamen on the bedplace and untie the ox hide.

"I called for Kigva," Spusscio says. "If anyone can save Ryamen, she can." Kigva lays her head on Ryamen's chest and listens, then peers intently into her eyes. She shakes her head and glares at us. "Poor thing. Is this Ogern's doing?"

I nod. "Yes. He must have taken her there seven days ago."

Spusscio says, "He would have kept her alive to try to learn what she knows about Lady Ilena."

"Hmpf! Barely alive, I'd say." She turns back to her patient and strokes her forehead. Her voice is tender as she continues, this time to Ryamen. "I'll try, old friend. We've had many bedside vigils together. This one I'll stand alone."

I blink back tears. There is no doubt Ryamen is in good hands.

Cormec speaks from the doorway. "Is there anything else, Spusscio?" He turns to me. "Lady?"

I shake my head.

Spusscio leaves the fire and joins Cormec. "Come

with me to Belert, if you will. We must tell him we've found Ryamen."

I watch for a time as Kigva tends Ryamen. She gives her a warm herb potion and watches carefully after each spoonful to be sure that Ryamen swallows it.

"Can I help?" I ask.

Kigva says, "No, lady. There is little to do but watch. I'll not leave her."

Ryamen's small house feels comfortable and safe. I am reluctant to leave, but I fear I am in the way here. "I'll look back in, then, from time to time," I say.

Kigva nods. "I'm sure Spusscio will also. I'll see that you're called if she awakens."

I look for a quiet place where I can be alone. The ladder to the ramparts is nearby, and I think of yesterday's struggle as I climb. Ogern's dirk against my neck and his strong arm binding my arms to my body are memories that won't fade for a long time.

The sky is cloudy, and there is a sharp wind off the sea. Last night Lenora spoke of snow, and those who rode with me from Dun Dreug prepare to leave at first light tomorrow. I try to keep walking past the place where Ogern fell, but something forces me to stop and look down to the rocks.

I glance quickly and look back at the sea. I realize that I didn't see a dark form below. I look again, this time carefully. The tide has risen during the night and washed the body away. It is a relief to know it is gone, but the picture of Ogern sprawled motionless on the rocks will haunt me forever.

I stroll along the walltop and let the sea wind carry my thoughts away.

Durant's voice startles me. "I've been looking for you."

I turn to face him. The pain still stabs when I look into his eyes. Soon he will leave to join his family, and I can try to forget him.

He seems uncertain of what he will say. He starts, "You have found what you sought."

"Perhaps," I say. "But I still don't know who my mother is, or why I was sent away."

"As chief of Dun Alyn, you have a place. And you will have suitors. Your choice, I suppose, of any man in Britain."

I don't want any man in Britain. I want only one. The sea wind buffets us, the surf roars below, and the bustle of the fortress seems far away. The idea that I could be a chief fades like a dream at daylight. The only realities here are the man beside me and the feelings I have for him.

He goes on. "I hoped, when you were without lineage or position, that you would come to care for me. I thought to ask you to journey to the South to meet my family."

I study his face. There is no pretense there. I wait for him to go on.

"But now I understand," he says, "that things have changed. You must think of Dun Alyn. And you will need to arrange a proper marriage. I have no large holdings, no great wealth. Hadel is a small fortress with barely fifty warriors at my call."

"Your family," I say. "What would they think of me?"

He smiles. "My mother would welcome you. And my son would love you."

I wait, but he says no more. At last I ask the question I have agonized over for days. "And your wife?"

He looks puzzled. "My wife is dead. She died five years ago when the child was born. Why did you think I had a wife?"

"I—" I stop. My face begins to burn from more than the wind. "I overheard Hoel mention your son, and I assumed . . ." I look down. He can have little doubt about my feelings now.

His voice is soft. I have to strain to hear it above the wind. "Is that why you changed? You avoided talking with me and hurried on when I tried to walk beside you."

I nod.

"I thought it was because you had found your true place. Because you knew it would be important to find a proper husband."

I shake my head, still without speaking. I don't trust my voice right now.

He reaches out and lifts my chin so my eyes meet

his. He speaks slowly, with deep feeling. "When my wife died, I thought that I would never care for another woman. That kind of loss is too cruel. When I met you, I began to think of marriage again."

I still dare not speak, but my eyes must tell him how I feel.

He continues, "I do not want a pledge from you now. You need time to learn what it means to rule Dun Alyn. Talk with Belert about the kind of marriage a chief should make."

"I will not make a marriage I do not want," I say.

He smiles. "Do not be hasty. There are many men in Britain. You may well meet one who drives me from your mind."

I shake my head. "I don't think so."

"Still, I want you to be sure. This is a difficult time for you. I will return when the snows melt from the passes. We will talk then. If you do not wish to marry me, I will always be your brother as I pledged."

"I will wait for you, then, in the spring." I want to say more, but I'm not sure just what.

"Ilena!" A shout comes up to us over the sound of the wind. It is Belert. "Come. Ryamen is awake."

CHAPTER 16

RYAMEN IS PROPPED UP ON A PILE OF BEDSKINS. HER FACE is still pale, but her eyes are open and alert. She makes a weak motion toward me. I reach out and clasp her dry hand with my own cold ones. She clutches my fingers firmly and does not release them when I try to let go.

The room is crowded. Kigva hovers over a tiny pot at the fire. Three I do not know—two men and a woman, all of Belert's age or older, all with an air of authority—sit on benches pulled close to the bedplace. Belert sets a small stool beside me and motions me to sit down. He takes a place on the bed, at Ryamen's feet. Durant stops at the door.

"Come on in, Durant," Belert says. "We have three here from Dun Alyn, but a witness from Arthur's table is more than welcome."

Durant finds a clear spot on the floor stones near the entrance and sits, leaning against the wicker wall.

"I feared for you." Ryamen's voice is stronger than I expected. The others shift and lean closer. She looks only at me. "I could not get back. Resad was at the gate when I tried to return to you."

"I was fine," I say. "You rescued me when I could not save myself and led me to shelter."

"You are your mother's child," she says.

The words do not alarm me. I know that she will not name Grenna as my mother, and I have no idea what she will tell us. Yet I am content here. I belong at Dun Alyn just as I belonged with Moren and Grenna in the Vale of Enfert. There is peace and safety in this room. I take a deep breath and settle myself on the stool.

The scent of herbs in the room brings thoughts of Grenna. It is thyme I smell, thyme and borage and something I don't recognize. But the thyme is strongest. Thyme wasn't known to the women in the Vale of Enfert, and Grenna couldn't find any in the fields around us. I remember Moren's return with Cryner. After the commotion I made over the new puppy, Moren pulled a parcel from his pack and handed it to Grenna.

"I brought you a gift also. From . . ." I remember how he started to name someone, then stopped and said, "From your good friend."

It was a bundle of thyme, dry and fragrant. Grenna tied a piece of cloth around the twigs to catch the seeds. When spring came, we planted thyme in the corner of our yard; it grows there still. I look around Ryamen's little room at the bundles and stacks of drying plants and understand now who sent that gift to Grenna.

An elder behind me, the woman, asks, "Tell us first, Ryamen, who put you into the pit and why."

"Resad and Ogern," Ryamen answers. "Only I know the truth of Ilena's birth. As long as I live, Ogern cannot claim Dun Alyn for his granddaughter. They will try again."

"No," Belert says. "Ogern and Resad are dead. Will you tell us what you know?"

The room is silent while she considers this. When she speaks, her voice is low. "Ogern was a good Druid in the old days. Resad fed his hunger for power." Her dark eyes move from one face in the room to another and settle on the elders. "Will you give oath to keep Ilena safe? Do you intend to honor Cara's wishes?"

I keep my eyes on her face and do not turn to look at those behind me. I hear their murmurs.

"The lady has nothing to fear from me."

"I pledge to carry out Cara's wishes in this matter, if we can determine them."

"Let us hear the truth, old woman."

Belert says, "I have told these elders, and will tell all in the Great Hall tonight, that Ilena is heir to Dun Alyn. As Moren's daughter she is the proper successor to Cara."

Ryamen looks at him in silence for a time, then brings her eyes back to me. "Ilena is not Moren's daughter."

It takes a few minutes to understand what she has said. I keep my eyes on hers and draw strength from her steady stare while I try to take in this new blow. In all the agony of accepting the news that Grenna is not my mother, I never even considered that Moren might not be my father.

The house in Enfert, so like this one, comes into my mind again. The love I knew there was the love of parents for a child. No matter what I learn now, when I hear the word "father," I will always picture Moren; and when I hear the word "mother," I will always see Grenna's kind face smiling at me.

There is a shifting behind me. Someone lets out a noisy breath. I can see Belert's face fall. It will be difficult to name me chief if the people of Dun Alyn are not satisfied that I am the true heir.

"Ilena . . ." She stops and closes her eyes.

Kigva pushes past me with a bowl of warm water. I try to release Ryamen's hand to move out of the way, but her grasp is firm. I lean to one side so the healer can work. She speaks softly to her patient. "You must go slowly, old one. Another would be dead by now. You are too weak to talk."

We wait while she bathes Ryamen's face with the cloth and adjusts the skins behind her back. When

Kigva moves out of the way, I free one hand and smooth Ryamen's brow with gentle strokes. Her eyes flutter open.

I say softly, "Can you speak now, Ryamen? If not, it can wait until you are stronger." My feelings are at war inside me. Part of me wants to know what she will say, but another part throws a fierce wall against the thought that Moren and Grenna are not my parents. Perhaps if she says no more, I can blot this nightmare out.

She turns her head slightly and focuses on my face. "I must speak now." Her voice is low, and I hear the ones behind me shift and rustle as they bend closer. "I promised Cara. Moren promised also, and he is gone. I must . . ." Her voice trails off.

Belert stands and sighs. "We should go. It is cruel to keep her from resting."

"Cruel? Cruel to keep me from speaking, Belert." Her voice is stronger. "Sit and wait." She seems to gather herself before our eyes, and she continues. "It was the end of the long winter. Belert was away. The birthing began."

There is total silence now in the crowded house.

She rests a moment, then goes on. "It was a hard birth. Grenna and I were with her." She closes her eyes again.

I hear one of the elders behind me whisper, "She is telling of Miquain's birth. She is confused."

I can see the frown on Belert's face as he turns to the speaker. It is quiet again.

Ryamen opens her eyes and continues in a steadier voice, "It was not her time, though she was very large. At last a baby was born, a beautiful girl."

There is an impatient rustle behind me and another glare from Belert.

Ryamen breathes deeply for a few moments before she speaks. "Grenna took the baby, and I started to press Cara's abdomen to force the afterbirth."

Belert's thoughts seem far away now. How painful this must be for him, with Cara and Miquain both gone.

"My lady screamed and stopped me. She tried to speak, but the birthing force took away her words. Another head appeared. It was a second baby girl."

"Twins!" The voice comes from behind me.

Belert is pale, and his face shows deep sorrow and a sudden understanding. "I was not there to protect her. She would have feared the old curse."

"Yes," Ryamen says. "She knew Ogern would act against the children. The taboo against twins was still strong then."

"I should have been with her," Belert says.

One of the men behind me speaks. "I remember that winter, Belert. You had no choice but to lead a hunt. People were hungry. I rode with you; game was scarce. We traveled for two days before we found anything."

Ryamen continues, "While I tended the second child, Grenna laid the first at her mother's breast and went for Moren."

"He stayed behind with a few others to guard Dun Alyn," Belert says. "And because Grenna was distraught about losing their own infant just two days earlier."

"Yes," Ryamen continues. "Cara and Grenna were so happy to be with child at the same time. And then Grenna's boy died a few hours after his birth."

"What did Moren propose?" Belert asks.

Ryamen sighs and closes her eyes. Kigva hurries to her. This time the bowl holds a potion with a sharp medicinal scent. I help hold Ryamen's head while she sips a few mouthfuls.

After a few moments she begins to speak again. "Moren wanted to stay with Cara to protect her and the babies. He said you would deal with Ogern when you returned."

"Yes. Would that I had faced him down many years ago." Belert sighs.

"Cara insisted that one of the girls be taken to safety at once. At last Moren agreed. He and Grenna hurried to prepare for a journey."

I try to grasp the meaning of what I am hearing, but it is too bewildering. I feel I must be deep in a dream.

"Cara held both tiny girls for a time, then she handed Miquain to me and sat with Ilena alone, sobbing bitterly."

I cannot hold back the tears myself now. The picture Ryamen paints is so beautiful and so sad that I cry from both love and sorrow. When I look at Belert, I see tears on his cheeks too.

"And so," the woman behind me says, "Cara sent the secondborn away to save her?"

"No." Ryamen's voice is firm now. She seems to gain strength from the telling. "She kept Miquain, the secondborn. Ilena, the firstborn, was stronger and more likely to survive a trip."

One of the men speaks behind me. "And so it is Miquain we would have sacrificed in the grove?"

Ryamen looks toward him. "Yes. And Ilena would have lived. She is the elder, the true heir of Dun Alyn. That is why my lady sent me to take the Great Torc of Dun Alyn from its hiding place. When Grenna took Ilena, Cara placed the torc on her wrappings. It is rightfully hers.

"Cara longed to see Ilena, but she knew from Moren's visits that the child was well. She sent gifts that Ilena would someday know came from her mother."

Belert looks at me and smiles a slow, sad smile. "So, you are not Miquain, but still you are my daughter."

I do not know how to answer. I understand what has been said, but I do not really feel the truth of the situation yet. I look into his eyes and return his smile. Two fathers! Moren and Belert!

Belert turns back to Ryamen. "Why didn't Cara tell me? She must have known I would fight for our children."

Ryamen answers, "She knew that well. She feared for her daughters, but she also feared for you. She was sure that Ogern would use the twins as an excuse to challenge you for Dun Alyn, and then you and both children would be in danger. She knew better than you what Ogern was capable of."

Durant stands and says, "I did not know any held twins to be a curse. I thought that idea died out everywhere generations ago."

Belert says, "It has not been practiced here in recent years. But at the time of Miquain's—and Ilena's—birth the Druids still sacrificed the secondborn twin of livestock and of humans."

An elder behind me says, "The lady Cara fought against that practice for years and finally stopped it."

"Hmph!" Kigva speaks from her place by the fire. "It is still practiced at times. Chiefs don't always know what Druids do."

"There will be no more human sacrifice at Dun Alyn—anywhere, by anyone!" The words burst from my mouth with such force that even I am surprised.

Belert stares at me for a moment and then nods. "Yes, Ryamen is right. You are your mother's daughter."

Ryamen's next words are soft and slow. "Cara made me pledge again, not long before her death, that I would tell the story when it was time. I was not in the hall the night Cormec brought Ilena in, but I heard about it from a neighbor on his way home from dinner.

I knew the time had come to speak, but first I wanted to get Ilena to safety."

"Thank you, Ryamen," Belert says. "You honor Cara's memory with your courage."

Ryamen manages another small smile and closes her eyes. Kigva moves to her side and speaks to Belert. "She is so weak. Are you through?"

He nods and stands. "Is there any doubt about Ilena's place at Dun Alyn?"

The three elders get up at the same time, and all gaze from my face to Belert's. The woman speaks. "There seems no doubt at all." She looks to the others.

"None. Ilena is the true chief of Dun Alyn." The speaker is the taller of the two men.

"We welcome you, Chief Ilena." The third elder to speak has a deep voice and a stern face. "We regret the dangers you have faced here."

"Thank you," I say. "I am unharmed, but"—I nod to Ryamen—"others have suffered for me."

The woman says, "We let Ogern influence us for too long."

We move out into the compound, and the elders make their farewell.

Durant says, "I must meet with Hoel and the others. We plan to leave at daybreak tomorrow."

"Will you be at dinner?" I ask.

"Of course," Durant says. "I want to see you dressed as a lady again. This time I can use both eyes." He nods to Belert and hurries off to the men's quarters.

Belert and I face each other in silence. I remind myself that he is my father. And I am Chief of Dun Alyn!

"Well, Ilena." He reaches out to touch my cheek with his finger. "Dun Alyn is yours now." He looks in the direction Durant has taken. "Someday you will choose a man to rule beside you."

I smile. "I'm sure I can find one."

"I will see you at dinner, then. People are eager to greet you. Will you wear the green dress again?"

"But I have . . ." I would prefer to wear my own, yet I want to please my father. "Of course, if you like. But I will wear the girdle that my mother made for me."

When I return to my quarters, I find my pack has been opened and things put away. My blue dress lies over the bedplace. I open the larchwood box and take out the green one. Why does Belert prefer the green? Perhaps he doesn't know I own a dress. He might like the blue as well.

The servant girl comes in. "I put away your things, lady. Will you wear the blue dress to the banquet?"

"I think the green," I say.

"Miquain wore it always," she says. "And she had another before it."

Suddenly I remember. Green is the ancient color worn by women who are priestesses or chiefs. In the old times no one else was allowed to wear green. It is still rarely worn by any but women of ruling families.

"The green," I say.

She takes up my blue shift and folds it neatly before placing it in the box. "If you are ready to bathe, I'll bring water," she says.

"I wish that I could wash my hair." I go to the window. The sun is out now, and it is warm. "Do I have time?"

"Of course. The ladies always washed their hair just outside in the yard. I'll bring warm water and a basin."

What luxury! With someone to pour water and fetch more when that is gone, the job goes quickly. We move inside for me to bathe and put on the green dress. Then I go back out and sit on a bench to comb the tangles while sun and wind dry my hair. I am enjoying the sensation of being clean all over when I hear a small voice behind me.

"Lady Ilena? May I talk with you?" It sounds like a child.

I turn to see the girl who sat beside Ogern in the Great Hall. It must be his granddaughter. She is pale and her eyes are red with weeping. She is holding her hands behind her back. I remember Ogern's body on the rocks and feel a wave of sorrow for the child.

"Of course," I say.

"I brought you this." She thrusts the torc into my lap and jumps back as if she is afraid I will strike her.

"Thank you," I say. "Did your mother or father tell you to bring it to me?"

Her voice is very soft, and she looks down at her feet as she answers. "I don't have a mother or father. They're dead. I only had Ogern."

I think of how I felt at Moren's death. "I'm sorry." I reach out to comfort her, but she moves back farther. "I won't hurt you," I say.

"Will you have me killed?" she asks.

"Of course not."

"Or send me away somewhere?"

"No. You are my cousin, and you belong here at Dun Alyn. I won't hurt you."

"Ogern wanted to hurt you. I know he did."

"That doesn't mean that I will hurt you."

"Thank you, lady." She gives me a last frightened look, then turns and runs out of the small courtyard.

The torc gleams in the sunlight. I trace the strange face-like carvings in the terminals with my finger. The Great Torc of Dun Alyn. I can almost see my mother, shadowy and indistinct, laying the neckpiece gently on the small bundle in Grenna's arms. My tears blur the gold into a blaze of light.

The Great Hall is as crowded and noisy as it was that night when Cormec led me, injured, frightened, and dirty, up to Belert's table. The carved chair is empty. Belert—my father—Lenora, and Perr are seated to its right; Durant, Hoel, and Doldalf are on its left. The bandage on Doldalf's shoulder is white above his checked tunic.

I peer through the smoky haze for a few minutes

before I realize that the place of honor in the center is for me. Lenora sees me and waves.

Heads turn throughout the hall, and the place falls silent. I smooth my girdle and resist the urge to adjust the circlet in my hair. The torc is warm against my neck as I take a deep breath and square my shoulders.

Grenna said, "There is a place the three of us belong. Someday we'll go there."

I start down the aisle between the tables and pretend for a few steps that she and Moren are walking beside me.

AFTERWORD

THE LEGEND OF LADY ILENA IS HISTORICAL FICTION. There is no mention of a young woman named Ilena in the stories that have come down from the Dark Ages. However, those old tales hold fascinating glimpses of life in the hill forts and village settlements of sixth-century Britain.

In a culture without writing, stories kept the records: family trees, tribal histories, records of crop successes and failures, reports of hunting trips, chronicles of alliances and battles. The stories were entertainment, a way to pass long evenings and forget for a time the hard work of the day and the danger all around, but they were also the newspapers, file cabinets, textbooks, and databases of the time. Every fortress of note had its own bard; every village had a storyteller.

Hero tales were especially popular, and legends about a warrior named Arthur have lasted until our own time. Fanciful romances have been written about a

King Arthur said to have lived during the late Middle Ages, A.D. 1000 to 1400. However, historians and archaeologists say that Arthur, if he existed at all, was the military leader who directed the resistance to Saxon invasions of Britain around A.D. 500.

I have set *The Legend of Lady Ilena* in northern Britain (now Scotland) in about A.D. 500. This was a time of great tumult in Britain. The Roman legions, which had brought central government and a stable society to southern Britain (now England), had been gone for more than a century. Old tribal rivalries broke out once more across the land. Germanic tribes (Saxons) invaded and occupied the Southeast, and Irish war bands plundered, took slaves, and ultimately began to settle in the West.

In the North tribes were faced with a difficult choice between continuing old feuds and making an alliance to stand against the Saxons, who were pushing ever north and west. Some tribes apparently joined with clans of the South to hold the line against the invaders. Others, however, allied with Saxons to fight their old enemies.

The new religion, Christianity, was spreading throughout Britain. People held on to most of their old beliefs when they accepted Christianity, but the Christian monks, because they opposed human sacrifice, were a threat to the power of the Druids. This added another layer to the complicated political and social interactions of the time.

The Druids had influenced Celtic society for centuries. In this time before science and modern medicine, people believed that gods and spirits intervened in human lives. The Druids, as the religious leaders, controlled the rituals and sacrifices that appeased those forces. The Druids were also custodians of the ancient legal codes. As the authorities in things that affected people's daily lives, they often had more power than the chiefs who ruled the fortresses.

Amid all this turmoil, the common people, who were very much like us, battled to save their homes, worked to feed and protect their families, and struggled to live honorable lives. Their stories continue to speak to us across the years and link us in spirit with the sixth-century Britons.

ABOUT THE AUTHOR

PATRICIA MALONE grew up on a farm in central Illinois. She has traveled extensively throughout Great Britain, researching its history, legends, and folktales. She is particularly interested in Scotland, the land of her ancestors.

Patricia Malone lives in Naperville, Illinois, and divides her time between writing and teaching. *The Legend of Lady Ilena* is her first novel.